"Let's have a bet, shall we?" said Mac.

A bet. The very word brought back a rush of memories. Their marriage had had an undercurrent of competition that had kept their relationship sparking, because no matter how frivolous, tender or erotic the challenge, the truth was that neither of them had ever liked to lose.

"So what's the bet this time?" Georgia asked as coolly as she could.

"I bet I can convince you that I love you and can be what you need," said Mac. "And, what's more, I bet I can make you realize that you still love me."

Georgia laughed. "Well, I bet you can't!"

"If I win, you tear up those papers and we stay married. If you win..." Mac shrugged. "I'll sign and the divorce will go straight through."

"Oh, this is ridiculous! We can't possibly make a bet like that!"

"Chicken?" said Mac provocatively.

Georgia glared at him. "Is there a time limit on this bet? I don't want to be hanging on indefinitely."

"Why don't we say three months?" suggested Mac.

Three months. She could easily hold out that long.

"All right." Georgia met his gaze squarely, her own bright with challenge. "You're on."

MARRIAGE REUNITED

Jessica Hart

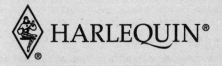

HARLEQUIN®

TORONTO • NEW YORK • LONDON
AMSTERDAM • PARIS • SYDNEY • HAMBURG
STOCKHOLM • ATHENS • TOKYO • MILAN • MADRID
PRAGUE • WARSAW • BUDAPEST • AUCKLAND

ISBN 0-373-18235-X

MARRIAGE REUNITED

First North American Publication 2006.

Copyright © 2006 by Jessica Hart.

All rights reserved. Except for use in any review, the reproduction or
utilization of this work in whole or in part in any form by any electronic,
mechanical or other means, now known or hereafter invented, including
xerography, photocopying and recording, or in any information storage
or retrieval system, is forbidden without the written permission of the
publisher, Harlequin Enterprises Limited, 225 Duncan Mill Road,
Don Mills, Ontario, Canada M3B 3K9.

All characters in this book have no existence outside the imagination of
the author and have no relation whatsoever to anyone bearing the same
name or names. They are not even distantly inspired by any individual
known or unknown to the author, and all incidents are pure invention.

This edition published by arrangement with Harlequin Books S.A.

® and TM are trademarks of the publisher. Trademarks indicated with
® are registered in the United States Patent and Trademark Office, the
Canadian Trade Marks Office and in other countries.

www.eHarlequin.com

Printed in U.S.A.

Jessica Hart was born in west Africa, and has suffered from itchy feet ever since—traveling and working around the world in a wide variety of interesting but very lowly jobs, all of which have provided inspiration to draw from when it comes to the settings and plots of her stories. Now she lives a rather more settled existence in York, U.K., where she has been able to pursue her interest in history, although she still yearns sometimes for wider horizons. If you'd like to know more about Jessica, visit her Web site www.jessicahart.co.uk

CHAPTER ONE

'THANK YOU for coming in. I'll be in touch.' Georgia closed the door firmly behind the latest applicant for the post of senior photographer on the *Askerby and District Gazette* and let the bright, polite smile drop from her face.

Mentally she began to compose a letter for Rose to type up and send to all five of the hopefuls who had responded to the advertisement.

Dear X, Thank you so much for coming in and wasting my time today. While admiring your nerve in applying for a job for which you have no experience and absolutely no talent, I am afraid that I am unable to offer you the post. I am desperate for a photographer, but not that desperate. Yours sincerely, Georgia Maitland, Editor.

What a shame you couldn't tell it how it was, instead of wrapping it in meaningless phrases, thought Georgia, already resigned to drafting a letter that would make her sound kind and encouraging instead of cross and impatient, which was how she really felt.

As if she didn't have enough to do.

Taking off her glasses, she dropped them on to her desk and threw herself into the battered executive chair with a gusty sigh, spinning round to face the window behind. The view over the rooftops of the town to the hills beyond was one of the few bonuses of the *Gazette*'s location on the third floor of a bleak Victorian warehouse which had been badly converted in the Seventies.

On this March afternoon, a weak winter sun was struggling to stay above the horizon and the hills, still dusted with snow from a cold snap earlier in the week, were reflecting a pinkish glow. It would make a nice picture, thought Georgia morosely.

If only she could find a photographer capable of taking it.

Behind her, she heard the door to her office open. This would be Rose, still struggling to learn the ropes as the *Gazette*'s secretary, and almost as anxious as Georgia to find a new photographer. She would be wanting to know how the last interview had gone.

'He seems terribly nice,' she had whispered to Georgia confidentially before ushering the last candidate in.

Nice he might have been, a talented photographer he most certainly wasn't.

'Please tell me that guy wasn't the best photographer Askerby can come up with,' Georgia said without turning round.

'I could tell you that if you want, but then I'd be lying, and you know I've never lied to you, Georgia.'

The voice that answered her was far from her secretary's cut-glass tones. Instead it was warm and amused, with a Scottish lilt that was more a softening of the hard edges than a full-blown accent.

It was a voice Georgia hadn't heard for four long years. A voice so unexpected and so bizarrely out of place in her dull provincial office that she froze for a moment, certain that she must be imagining things.

Then, very, very slowly, she swivelled her chair round to face her husband.

'Hello, Georgia,' he said.

Georgia's heart, which had lurched into her throat at the sound of his voice, did a series of spectacular somersaults before landing with a sickening thud that left her reeling and breathless.

Mac Henderson, the love of her life. The man she had married. The man who had broken her heart.

The first instinctive surge of joy at the sight of him was rapidly succeeded, much to Georgia's relief, by a welcome rush of therapeutic anger. It was typical of Mac to turn up when she was least expecting him!

Just when she had managed to convince herself that she was over him.

How dared he come here looking just the same, with the same heart-shaking smile and the same unsettling humour gleaming in his navy-blue eyes, making her senses pirouette and her bones dissolve exactly the same way they always had?

It wasn't fair.

Georgia took a deep breath and wished she could remember some of those calming yoga exercises she had once tried.

'Mac,' she said, hating the way shock had made her voice husky, although, to be fair, it was a miracle she was able to speak at all given the way her heart was carrying on, cavorting around her ribcage like a red setter out of control. 'What are you doing here?'

'Looking for you.'

Mac looked as if he would have liked to have strolled around, but her office simply wasn't big enough for him to do more than take a couple of steps in any direction.

There you go, Georgia told herself. Another bonus to add to the view.

In the end, Mac sat down uninvited in the chair recently vacated by the would-be photographer. 'It took me a little while to track you down,' he said. 'You didn't tell me that you'd left London.'

'Is there any reason why I should have done?' asked Georgia coolly.

'We *are* married,' he pointed out.

'Technically, perhaps,' she conceded, 'but we've been separated for nearly four years and, since you haven't made any other attempt to contact me in that time, it didn't occur to me to keep you informed of my movements.'

Hey, who would have thought she would have been able to come up with a coherent sentence like that? Georgia marvelled. Who needed yoga anyway? She could do this. She could deal with her soon-to-be ex-husband without falling apart or letting the frantic churning get the better of her. Ha!

'I don't recall you letting me know whenever you went off to the Middle East or Angola or Liberia or all the other trouble spots you've been to over the last few years,' she added, feeling more confident now.

'You've been keeping track of me?'

The undercurrent of amusement in Mac's voice made Georgia grit her teeth. He had never really taken her seriously, and it looked as if nothing had changed.

'I read the papers,' she said, managing a careless shrug. 'I see your name under the pictures so I know where you've been, that's all.'

And every time it had been like a knife turning in her heart, knowing that he was in danger, never getting a phone call to say that he was safe, knowing only that he had survived one conflict the next time his photographs of another appeared in the paper.

Of course, Mac had always thrived on risk. His was an odd mixture of recklessness and competence, a confidence bordering on arrogance that he could deal with any obstacle that stood between him and a good picture.

It was what made him a wonderful photographer and a terrible husband. How many nights, Georgia wondered, had she lain awake worrying about where he was and what he was doing, only for him to breeze back, to laugh at her fears and tell her that she should learn to live dangerously, life was so much more fun that way? But it hadn't been fun for Georgia, just waiting for him to come home. He had never understood how hard it was for her.

She looked across the desk at him now. No, he hadn't changed. Nobody could call Mac a handsome man, his features were too irregular for that, but he was undeniably attractive, with those dark, lean looks, and that reckless, good-humoured assurance that gave his mobile face its compelling charm.

He was a little thinner now, maybe, a little more battered around the edges, but then, weren't they all? Georgia thought wryly. You didn't have to spend your life in war-torn countries to lose your sheen after you hit forty.

He had aged better than she had, she had to acknowledge, but then men always did. Mac's lines made him look rugged and humorous, hers just made her look tired and tense.

'Besides,' she went on, abandoning that depressing line of thought, 'I *am* a journalist. It wouldn't have been that hard to have found you if I'd needed to, which I haven't until now. I sent the divorce papers care of the Picture Desk at the paper. I presume that's why you're here?'

'Got it in one,' said Mac, not feeling nearly as casual as he sounded.

Her letter had been forwarded to him in Mozambique. He had been sitting in a bar in Maputo, having collected the mail that had accumulated in his post box while he'd been covering a story up country. He had ordered a beer while he leafed through the letters, opening anything that seemed interesting and leaving the rest until later.

Mac remembered the moment exactly. Remembered frowning slightly at the solicitor's stamp, turning the envelope over, ripping it open with his thumb. Even at the time he'd thought of Georgia, who would undoubtedly have used a letter opener or a knife to open it neatly rather than leave a jagged tear like that. It was the kind of memory that would catch at him like barbed wire, just when he least expected it.

He remembered shaking the thought of her aside as he'd pulled out the papers and unfolded them, remembered the sickening jolt as he'd read the solicitor's covering letter and the words sank in. After all this time, Georgia wanted a divorce.

'I appreciate the effort,' she said now in a dry voice, 'but there was no need for you to come. All you had to do was sign the papers and send them back to my solicitor.'

'But I don't want to sign,' said Mac, tipping the chair back so that he was balanced alarmingly on the back legs. 'I want to talk.'

'There's nothing to talk about,' said Georgia, trying to ignore his balancing act and failing miserably. 'And stop doing that!' she snapped, succumbing to the blatant provocation in spite of herself. 'You're only doing it to wind me up anyway. You know I hate it when you take stupid risks.'

'Georgia, I'm only sitting on a chair!' Mac rolled his eyes, but let the chair legs drop back to the floor.

'You're the only person I know who can sit on a chair dangerously,' she said with a trace of resentment and he grinned.

'That almost sounds as if you still care about me!'

'Well, I don't,' said Georgia, not quite truthfully. 'It's nothing to me if you want to break your neck. Just don't do it in my office when I'm trying to work!'

'You're not working now,' Mac pointed out. 'We're just talking.'

'We're *not* talking,' she insisted crossly. 'What is there to talk about?'

'Our marriage.'

'Mac, we don't *have* a marriage.' Georgia sighed. 'We agreed to separate four years ago. It was a mutual decision and since neither of us has changed our mind since then, there doesn't seem much point in carrying on being married on paper only. Surely you can see that it's sensible to sort everything out now?'

Sensible. There was a word to describe Georgia, thought Mac, studying her over the desk. She looked tired, he decided, and there were new lines around her smoky-grey eyes, but her blonde hair was still drawn neatly away from her face in a French plait, and she was as immaculately groomed as ever, wearing one of those little suits that always made her look crisp and elegant and just a little buttoned up.

The contrast in the two sides of Georgia had always intrigued him. There was the cool, controlled Georgia who faced the world, and then there was the other, much more alluring Georgia who shed her inhibitions with her neat suit and her sensible shoes, whose smile as she shook her beautiful hair free of its tidy plait had never failed to send a *frisson* of excitement down his spine.

Look at her now, sitting at her perfectly organised desk, crisp and capable in a scoop-necked silk top and discreet earrings. Who could guess that behind that practical façade was a warm, vibrant, alluring woman? Mac liked to think that he was the only one who knew, the only who had glimpsed the potential in the steady, sensible girl who had escaped the confines of a small Yorkshire town for London all those years ago, the only one to be fascinated and infuriated by her in equal measure.

The realisation that he might not be the only one after all had brought him all the way back from Mozambique, jealousy churning in his gut.

The amusement evaporated from Mac's face. 'The thing is, Georgia, you said that neither of us had changed our mind, but that's not quite true. I have.'

She stared at him. 'What do you mean, you've changed your mind?'

'About being better off apart than together. I don't think that any more.' The navy-blue eyes looked directly into hers. 'I don't want a divorce.'

For one long, long moment Georgia couldn't say anything at all. She was too busy struggling to control her wayward heart which, contrary to all its hard training over the past four years, had done the equivalent of leaping to its feet and punching the air with an exhilarated *yes!*

How pathetic was *that*? All those tears, all that heartache. The pain, the confusion, the desolation...she had got over it all. She had survived, she was *over* him, and now all her body could do was thrill at the mere suggestion that he might, after all, still want her.

Georgia was disgusted with herself. Well, her heart could do what it liked, but her will was stronger now—it had had to be—and she had absolutely no intention of going back to the arguments and the disappointments and the being taken for granted. It had taken her a long time to recover and be ready to move on. This was not the time to slide back down the slippery slope of desire, however sweet and seductive it might be.

'You may not want a divorce, Mac, but I do,' she said, hoping that her face didn't show the turmoil inside her. 'We've been perfectly happy separated for the last four years. What's the point of us staying married?'

'What's the point of us getting divorced?' he countered.

Tension began to tug at the edge of Georgia's eye, in spite of her best efforts to stay calm. That tic was a bad habit, one she thought she had kicked along with their marriage.

She could feel the old familiar frustration uncoiling inside her, leaving her taut and jittery. She had tried so hard to get rid of that feeling. Yoga, Pilates, relaxation classes, exercise…all utterly pointless when all it took was for Mac to walk into the room to bring it all back.

Breathe deeply, Georgia told herself. Don't let him get to you. You're forty-one, a professional woman, and you don't need to prove anything to anyone, least of all Mac.

'I want to move on,' she said as calmly as she could.

'Move on?' Mac echoed, raising derisive brows. 'What's that supposed to mean?'

'You know what it means, Mac.' Georgia had to clamp down hard on the irritation that threatened to boil over. She was *not* going to let this descend into one of their old, circular arguments.

'Look, *we agreed*,' she reminded him. 'We wanted different things, and neither of us was prepared to compromise, so we decided to separate, and we've both led our own lives since then. We should have got divorced four years ago, but it was difficult with you away so much and, since nobody else was involved, there didn't seem any particular reason to go through all the hassle of a divorce.'

'But now there is?' said Mac in a hard voice.

'Yes.' Georgia let out a breath. 'Yes, there is. My life has changed.'

'So it seems.'

Mac looked pointedly around her cramped office, with its dreary beige walls, old-fashioned filing cabinets, chipped desk and its view through the one glass wall of a newsroom so dated that it was almost a surprise to see computers instead of antiquated typewriters on the desk.

Georgia followed his gaze, knowing that he was remembering the newsroom in the national newspaper where she had worked in London, all steel and glass and technology and endlessly ringing phones. Did he have any idea how trapped she felt here?

'Why Askerby?' he asked abruptly. 'It's the last place I expected to find you. You couldn't wait to get away, and it was only guilt that brought you back to sort out family problems. Every time you came home, you'd breathe a sigh of relief to be back in London.'

It was true. She had never wanted to come back and live in Yorkshire, but sometimes you didn't have a choice.

'I had my reasons,' she said in a restrained voice.

His expression hardened. 'To do with the little boy you've adopted?'

'Yes, Toby. You remember him, don't you?'

Expecting her to be defensive about her adopted child, Mac was thrown. 'No...Toby? Who's Toby?'

'He's Becca's son.'

He might have known Becca would have been

behind all this. Mac remembered Georgia's sister all right. Talk about chalk and cheese. Becca was wild and chaotic, Georgia cool and determined. Forever held up as a contrast to her clever, ambitious sister, Becca had, perhaps inevitably, taken to her role as the black sheep of the family with gusto.

He sighed with exasperation. 'What's Becca up to now?'

With Becca you could never tell. She might be in prison, or simply have abandoned her child to go off and live in a commune, and either way it would no doubt fall to Georgia to clean up the mess she had left behind her. Becca had always relied on Georgia to help her out of whatever trouble she was in. Mac hadn't liked the emotional blackmail she had exerted, implying that it was somehow Georgia's fault that she hadn't made a success of her life.

'Just let her sort it out herself,' he used to tell Georgia. 'She'll never learn to look after herself if she knows all she has to do is pick up the phone to you when things go wrong. I'd let her stew.'

But Georgia never would. 'She's my sister,' she would protest, but Mac knew she felt guilty about being their parents' favourite, guilty about having the brains and the beauty, guilty about the fact that Becca had never really been able to struggle out from under her shadow.

And now it seemed Becca never would.

'She's dead,' said Georgia tonelessly.

Mac stared at her, shocked. '*Dead*? How? What happened?'

Georgia sighed and ran her fingertips under her eyes. 'A car accident. She'd been out at a night-club in Leeds, and she'd been drinking. She should never have been driving at all, but you know Becca.' Shaking her head, she blew out a breath. 'It was just fortunate that no one else was involved. Sometimes she could be so…so…'

'Irresponsible?' Mac suggested, watching Georgia's hands clenching and unclenching with frustration.

Her grey eyes met his and then slid away. 'She was my sister, and I loved her, but sometimes I feel so angry with her for what she's done to Toby,' she confessed in a low voice, not looking at him.

'It's normal to feel angry at times when you're grieving,' said Mac in a matter-of-fact voice. 'You shouldn't feel guilty about it.'

He was wasting his breath, of course. He didn't need to look at her face to know that. Georgia was bound to feel guilty. She always had felt guilty about Becca, and Becca dying wasn't going to change that.

'I'm sorry about Becca, Georgia,' he said sincerely. 'It must have been a shock for you.'

'Yes.' Georgia remembered that terrible phone call, more than a year ago now. Her mother's distress had been so acute that it had taken ages before Georgia could understand what had happened and, when she had finally grasped what her mother was trying to tell her, she had known at once that her life would never be the same again.

'Yes, it was,' she said. 'It was terrible, but not as terrible as it was for Toby. He was only seven, and he'd lost his whole world. Becca might have been irresponsible, but she did love him, and she was his mother. No one else will ever be able to take her place.'

'But you're trying?'

Georgia looked up at that. 'I'm doing the best I can,' she said quietly. 'But it's never going to be enough.'

'Why you?' asked Mac after a moment. 'Where's Toby's father?'

'Who knows?' Georgia lifted her shoulders helplessly. 'I don't think Becca did. He took off before Toby was born, and she never tried to find him. Even if it were possible to somehow track him down, I couldn't hand Toby over to a perfect stranger. That's why I adopted him.'

Mac shifted restlessly in his chair. He wanted to get up and prowl around, but the office was simply too small, so he was stuck there, struggling to assimilate what she had told him. It was totally unreasonable to resent Georgia for doing the right thing by her nephew, but he still did. He didn't like the fact that she had gone ahead and changed her life for her sister's child when she hadn't been prepared to change it for a child of his.

He didn't like himself for not liking it. He knew he was being unfair and unkind and unreasonable.

But that was how he felt.

'What about your mother?' he said. 'Couldn't she have taken Toby?'

'She couldn't cope, Mac. She used to babysit him when Becca went out, but he was really too much for her. And anyway—' Georgia stopped as she felt her voice wobble treacherously.

Damn Mac. There was something about him that brought all her emotions to the surface and left her feeling raw and vulnerable. She hadn't cried for ages, and she wasn't about to start again in front of him.

Fiercely swallowing down the tears, she cleared her throat. 'Anyway,' she said again, more strongly this time, 'Mum never got over the shock of Becca's accident. She had a fatal stroke three months later.'

'Oh, Georgia.' Mac half rose out of the chair, then checked himself. Her father had died before they were married, and it was Georgia who had supported her mother and sister ever since.

He looked at her sitting behind her desk, her chin lifted defensively as if to ward off any attempts at sympathy for the fact that she had recently lost all her family. And he hadn't been there to help her through any of it.

'I'm sorry,' he said inadequately.

Georgia gave a brief smile of acknowledgement, and then went on. 'Mum did her best with Toby, and I came down every weekend, but it wasn't really working, and the social services were suggesting that they tried to find him a foster family when she died. I was due to have a meeting with them after the funeral, but I just looked at Toby that morning and realised I couldn't go through with it. I was the only family he had—and he was the only family I had.'

Her eyes darkened with the memory of those dreadful days. 'I told them that I would take him.'

'So that's why you're here in Askerby?' said Mac after a moment.

She nodded. 'I tried taking Toby to London, but he hated it. I had a super-cool loft apartment by the Thames, but no garden and there were no other children there. He was miserable at school and childcare arrangements were a nightmare…

'Toby just closed down,' she told him, shuddering at the very memory. 'He stopped talking, and I realised I was either going to have to give up on him or give up on my career.'

She mustered a smile and looked at Mac. 'I didn't really have a choice. He's been better ever since I brought him back. I'd sold Mum's house, but I've bought a new one, and he's back at his old school. I thought I might have to try free-lancing, but then I got this job…and look at me now.' She waved grandly around her tiny office, her expression ironic. 'I always did want to be an editor.'

Of a national newspaper, maybe. Georgia's plans had never included a dusty little local rag like this, Mac knew. She had given up a lot for Toby.

'It can't have been easy for you,' he offered. 'We all thought you were going far and that you would be editor of *The Times* at least by now!'

'Oh, come now, why would I want *The Times* when I can have all this?' said Georgia with a wry smile. Through the glass wall she could see the shabby newsroom whose only occupant, Kevin, the sports reporter, was leaning back in his chair reading a tabloid. God only knew where the others were. They seemed to drift in and out at will, as far as Georgia could make out.

The sense of torpor that hung over the place depressed her anew, and Mac's presence only made the contrast with her previous life the crueller. He sat there exuding recklessness and an exotic mix of danger and glamour that belonged with breaking news and rush of adrenalin, the sense of being where important things were happening and news was being made, not just reported.

Mac looked as out of place in this dull, provincial office as she felt. He didn't have to be here, though, and she did. It wasn't about what she wanted any more. Toby came first now, she reminded herself fiercely.

But, oh, there were times when she longed to wake up and find that it was all a bad dream and that she was back at the newsdesk in London, two phones at each ear and emails from around the world bombarding her inbox, with the clock ticking towards the deadline and the whole office buzzing with excitement.

Georgia suppressed a sigh and focused on Mac once more. 'This is my life now,' she said, wishing she could sound more excited and positive about it. 'I've accepted that I need to make a new life here in Askerby, and I can't do that as long as I'm legally married to you.'

'You've met someone else.' It was a statement rather than a question.

She hesitated, although she couldn't think why. 'Yes,' she said after the tiniest of pauses.

'And you want to get married again?' he asked in an abrasive voice.

'No.' She shook her head firmly, surprised at the way she had instinctively recoiled at the very idea of marrying anyone else.

Although, if she was honest, marriage was probably what Geoffrey had in mind. Georgia wasn't prepared to go that far just yet, though.

'There's no question of marriage at the mo-

ment,' she said. 'It's true that I've met someone…a nice man who cares for me and who I
think can offer me what I need, but it doesn't
seem fair to embark on a serious relationship with
him until I've resolved things with you. He's
made me realise that by always putting off the
idea of divorce I've never really moved on, and
that's what I think I need to do now.'

Mac began to feel a little better. It didn't sound
as if this so-called 'serious relationship' had got
very far. It was typical of Georgia to want to play
fair and start a new relationship uncluttered by
baggage from the old one—she always did like
things tidy—but this man, whoever he was,
couldn't be that keen if he was prepared to hang
around and wait until she had sorted everything
out.

'Who *is* this guy?' he demanded, wondering
why the man didn't just sweep Georgia off her
feet, the way he would do.

The way he *had* done, he remembered.

'I don't think he's any of your business,' said
Georgia with a quelling look. Mac had met
Geoffrey once, soon after they were married, and
it couldn't be said that the two of them had got
on. It was hard to imagine two men more different
from each other, in fact.

Typically, Mac wouldn't let it go. 'Do I know
him? Who would you know in Askerby?' He
leant back in his chair once more, tipping dan-

gerously, and pulled his upper lip down in an effort of memory, until it struck him. 'Ah…I know! 'It's that guy who always pined after you, isn't it? The one who came to dinner once when we were staying with your mother? Bit of a stuffed shirt?'

Georgia's lips tightened, annoyed. Geoffrey could be a bit stuffy sometimes, but she had no intention of admitting that to Mac.

'He's a very nice man,' she said defensively. 'He's been incredibly kind since I moved back here.'

'What was his name again?' asked Mac. 'Gerald? Jeremy? Jim?'

'Geoffrey,' said Georgia coldly, knowing that if she didn't tell him Mac was more than capable of going on speculating with more and more ridiculous names all night.

'Geoffrey! That's it.' Mac seemed pleased to have had that little puzzle solved for him. He eyed Georgia narrowly. 'Well, well…so Geoffrey's your new man? You know, I wouldn't have said that he was exactly your type, Georgia.'

'Maybe I've changed,' she said with a certain defiance. 'I don't see what it has to do with you, anyway. To be honest, I could just wait another year and the divorce would come through automatically, but I thought we could be civilized about the whole thing. I can't believe you seriously want to stay married. You certainly never had any interest in being married before!'

Mac's brows snapped together at that and he let the chair drop abruptly to the floor once more. 'That's not true!'

'Isn't it?' Georgia met his look directly. 'Oh, I dare say you didn't mind having a wife who waited at home and dealt with things while you were away. It was easy for you to drop everything and go when there was someone there to pay the bills and get the boiler fixed and have some milk in the fridge when you came home, but you could get all that from a good housekeeping service. You weren't interested in being married to *me*.'

The lazy humour had vanished from Mac's face, to be replaced by a grimness she had never seen before. 'Of course I was interested in you!' he protested, rather white about the mouth. 'I loved you!'

'But what did you love, Mac? Oh, the sex was great, I'll give you that, but the rest of the time I'm not sure you even *saw* me. How much did you know about what I thought and what I felt and what I wanted? It was wonderful when we were first married,' she acknowledged, 'but after a while you started to take me for granted, and you forgot about me.'

'How could I forget you? You were my wife!'

'Exactly, and that's *all* I was. I was just your wife, someone who was always there, someone you could always rely on, who could see what needed to be done and got on and did it without making a fuss because what was the point? Someone had to do it, after all. I knew your job meant that you had to go away at a moment's notice, but after a while it began to seem that my only role was to support you, and that wasn't enough for me.'

She stopped and made herself breathe slowly, fighting down the old resentment. Mac had never understood this.

'I needed you to look at me and *see* me, see how I'd changed and what I could do for myself, not just for you,' she said quietly. 'But you never did.'

'I knew you better than anyone else,' he said, a muscle jumping in his jaw.

'You knew me as I was when we got married,' Georgia agreed, 'but you didn't know me when we separated, and you don't know me now. It's not *me* that you want at all. You want the Georgia you married,' she told him, 'but you can't have her. She doesn't exist any more.'

CHAPTER TWO

'YOU'RE just being a dog in the manger,' Georgia went on, warming to her theme. 'You haven't wanted me for the past four years, but you don't want anyone else to have me either. And please don't try telling me that you've been faithful to my memory!' She fixed Mac with a clear look. 'Journalists are a gossipy lot, and I know all about your girlfriends.'

Faint colour tinged his cheekbones. 'I'm not going to pretend I've been celibate for four years. Yes, there have been women, but I didn't love any of them the way I loved you and, God knows, I tried.'

'Oh, thanks, that's very reassuring!'

'I'm trying to be honest,' said Mac with obvious restraint. 'I know we both agreed we would be happier on our own, but that doesn't mean that I didn't feel hurt and bitter about the way things had ended. I wanted to meet someone else, someone I could love, someone who wanted children too, but the harder I tried to forget you, the more I found myself missing you. I'd meet someone young and beautiful and gentle, she'd be good with children and longing to have a family of her own, and all I could think about was you.'

He sounded almost angry about it.

'I did everything I could to get you out of my head. Over and over again, I reminded myself about your annoying habits, the way you drove me mad with your lists and your routines and the way you always had to be at the airport four hours early.'

But then he would remember her sensuality and her intelligence and her honesty, the kindness she kept concealed behind that brisk façade.

And, more treacherously still, he would remember her perfume, her warmth and her softness and the tickle of that glorious hair as she leant over to kiss him. Even now the very thought of it could make his whole body clench with desire.

'So you were always there, whether I wanted you or not,' he went on, resigned. 'I went a bit crazy after you left. I threw myself into work. The more dangerous the story was, the more I wanted to go. I got myself sent on a long assignment in Africa, but even that couldn't dislodge you from my mind. The thought of you just wouldn't go away. In the end I gave up,' he said simply. 'I decided it was always going to be you.'

Georgia bit her lip. She had been through the long, weary process of trying to shake off a haunting memory herself.

'If you felt like that about me, why didn't you do anything about it?' she challenged him, her grey eyes bright and direct. The last thing she wanted was to start identifying with him!

'I've only reached that conclusion recently,' he said, picking his words with care now. 'I could have come back, but I think part of me was afraid to change the balance of things. I used to hear about you occasionally. I knew you were doing well and I guess the fact that you never did anything about a divorce made me think it might be better to leave things as they were until I finished my assignment and could try and see if we could have another go.'

'In fact, I'm fitting conveniently into your schedule,' said Georgia in a withering voice.

That was typical! She had spent her whole marriage waiting for Mac's attention, waiting for him to finish one assignment, waiting for him to shake off the memories of some bitter, dreadful conflict that consumed him when he came home, hoping for a moment when he could stop thinking about what he had seen and think about her instead. But the call to the next war, the next disaster, the next misery had always come first.

'No.' Mac's jaw tightened. 'I got your letter, and that changed everything. I can make a living as a freelance, so I resigned and came home to find you. There was no way I was going to stay

in Africa and let you divorce me without a word
of explanation.'

'I have explained!'

'Not in a way that I can understand,' said Mac.
'I want to talk.'

Georgia regarded him crossly. It never occurred
to him to think about what *she* wanted!

This was her new life, and she didn't want him
here, reminding her of what she had left in
London, reminding her of the kind of person she
used to be, leaving memories and associations behind after he had gone. He changed things just by
walking into a room. Now she would never be
able to look at that stupid chair he kept tipping
back in without thinking of him.

'I can't talk now,' she said irritably. 'I'm busy.'

Mac lifted a disbelieving eyebrow and looked
into the newsroom where Kevin now had his feet
on the desk while he checked his mobile phone.

Georgia gritted her teeth. 'I've got a lot to do,
even if no one else does!'

'You were just staring out of the window when
I came in,' Mac pointed out unfairly.

'I was thinking!'

'Well, I'm not going to sign any papers until
we *have* talked some more,' he said, 'so when do
you suggest we meet?'

Georgia could feel her shoulders tighten with
tension. It was just like Mac to go on and *on* and
on until he got what he wanted. He just never

gave up. His persistence had won him some fantastic pictures, but it was a less appealing quality on an emotional level.

Really, she had more than enough problems at the moment without Mac strolling in and unsettling her, Georgia thought with a mixture of exasperation and weariness. It had always been the same. He would turn her world upside down, make a mockery of her attempts to stay cool and calm, send her senses spinning. She had hated the way he could make her feel wild and abandoned and out of control.

She had loved it too, a small part of Georgia acknowledged.

But not any more. She had changed, she reminded herself sternly. She had other priorities now, and they didn't include resurrecting a doomed relationship.

Georgia wished that Mac would just go, but she knew him well enough to know that he wouldn't move until he got what he wanted. Well, let him talk if he wanted to. She had made the decision to move on and change her life, and she wasn't about to change her mind now, no matter what he might have to say.

She might as well get it over and done with.

'Come to supper tonight,' she said with a sigh. It was lucky that she had already invited Geoffrey. Geoffrey was safe and solid and reliable. His very presence would remind her of all that was good about the new life she was choosing and all that was bad about her life with Mac.

Putting on her glasses, she pulled a pad of paper towards her and wrote out her address in her characteristically neat script.

'As you've tracked me down this far, I'm sure you won't have a problem finding your way,' she said as she tore off the sheet and handed it to Mac.

'Thanks,' he said, and twirled the paper between his fingers with a smile that Georgia only just managed to steel herself against in time. 'What time?'

He was always late. That was the one reliable thing about Mac, she thought, just as she could always rely on Geoffrey to be on time. She had asked Geoffrey for eight o'clock, when Toby went to bed, so they would have some time together before Mac turned up.

'Come at eight,' she said.

Mac got easily to his feet. 'Shall I bring anything with me?'

'Just the divorce papers,' said Georgia coolly. 'Preferably signed.'

She waited until the door had shut behind him before she groaned and dropped her head on to the desk with a thump. What *was* it with life at the moment? She'd no sooner struggle over one hurdle than another would be dropped in her way.

Ever since Becca had died, it had been one

thing after another. Adjusting her life around a small boy. Giving up the job she loved so much. Leaving London. Dealing with hostility over her appointment as editor here. Staff walkouts. And now Mac, thinking that he could stroll in here and take up where he'd left off!

Well, he would learn that he was wrong, thought Georgia with grim determination. She had listened to 'I will survive' and now she could sing along with Gloria Gaynor with the best of them. She *had* survived, and she was going to go on surviving. She had enough to worry about without Mac.

Of course, it was typical of him to come back now, just when she was getting her life under control, she reflected bitterly. But he would find that she had changed. She was stronger now, more sure of herself, and she had learned to manage perfectly well without him.

It had taken her four long years to get to this stage, though, and it had been a hard process. There was no way she was going through all that again, no matter how tantalising his smile might be. She was a professional woman, with a career and a life of her own. She didn't need him and she didn't want him.

Now all she had to do was convince her treacherous body of that. Particularly her heart, springing around like a boisterous puppy, and those legs, whose bones had dissolved at the mere sound of his voice… They were just going to have to shape up, Georgia thought as she lifted her head from the desk.

And as for her stupid senses, who knew no better than to start throwing a ticker tape parade, cheering the good memories as they marched victoriously past Georgia's puny defences—well, they could just pipe down too. Her head was in charge now.

Unconsciously, Georgia stiffened her spine. That was better. She was *not* going to let Mac cast her into confusion and turmoil the way he had before. She had other problems to deal with and more important things to consider, Toby chief among them. Let Mac have his say tonight, if that was what he wanted, but he would just have to accept that she had moved on and that her own need was for a very different life now.

Surely he would be able to accept it when he saw how much she relied on Geoffrey now?

Which reminded her; she ought to ring Geoffrey and warn him that Mac was coming for dinner. Geoffrey was about as different from Mac as it was possible to be. The Y chromosome was about all they had in common, Georgia thought ruefully, so while Mac might like surprises and living on the edge, Geoffrey most certainly didn't. He would want to be prepared.

Georgia settled her glasses back on her nose and immediately felt more businesslike. Reaching for the phone, she braced herself to deal with Geoffrey's PA, Ruth, who controlled access to her boss with a steely efficiency and a crisp manner that even Georgia found intimidating.

Sure enough, her attempt to speak to Geoffrey was immediately stonewalled by Ruth. 'I'm afraid he's with a client,' she said, and Georgia knew better than to ask her to interrupt the meeting.

She had often thought that Ruth's talents were wasted on a mere chartered surveyor. She should have been guarding the office of a Cabinet Minister at least. In fact, Rose could do with picking up a few tips from Ruth, Georgia reflected wryly. It might not be so easy then for the likes of Mac Henderson to stroll in and out of her office. No way would Mac have got past Ruth!

'Can I take a message?' Ruth was always polite, but Georgia sensed that she didn't like her. Georgia wasn't sure whether she was jealous of her relationship with Geoffrey or, in common with a good many other locals, resented her appointment as editor of the *Askerby and District Gazette*.

Probably both, thought Georgia wearily.

'No, it's all right, thanks, Ruth,' she said, unwilling to launch into an explanation of the fact that someone who was technically her husband was coming to dinner. She could just imagine how Ruth would react to *that* little bit of information! 'Just remind Geoffrey that I'm expecting him at eight tonight, would you?'

'There won't be any need for that,' said Ruth primly. 'He has eight written in his diary.'

In other words, dinner with Georgia was just another appointment for Geoffrey.

Biting back a retort, Georgia put down the phone and took off her glasses once more so that she could rub her eyes. She was fed up with today. She would write the leader tomorrow morning. It wasn't as if it would change anything. People in Askerby knew what they thought, and they weren't going to have any jumped-up journalist from London tell them any different.

It was hard to believe that she had grown up here sometimes. The ex-editor of the *Gazette* had been very popular locally, never mind that he had brought the paper to its knees, and few people were prepared to extend a welcome to Georgia when she was appointed in his place.

Geoffrey had been a notable exception, and she would always be grateful to him for that.

Although perhaps *grateful* wasn't the best way to describe how you felt about a man you were seriously considering having a relationship with?

Georgia pushed that particular worry aside impatiently. Really, she had too much else to think about now. One thing about Mac's reappearance—it would convince Geoffrey that she needed to finalise her divorce once and for all before she could contemplate embarking on another serious relationship.

She gave her email a final check and cast a quick eye over the agency reports in case anything dramatic had happened. Not that there would be much she could do about it if there were, she thought bitterly. Nobody in Askerby wanted *news* in their paper.

Her last job was to tidy her desk. She hated coming into a mess in the morning. Mac had used to call her a control freak but, if she was, she didn't seem to be a very good one, Georgia had long ago decided. If she was so controlling, how come life so often seemed to be completely out of her control?

Shrugging on her coat, she went out into the outer office, aware, as always, of the tiny moment of silence that fell whenever she appeared.

'I'm off now, Rose,' she said, hating the way her voice sounded a little too hearty, a little too much as if she were trying too hard not to mind how long it was taking her to be accepted. 'Don't forget the editorial conference tomorrow morning. I want everyone there.'

'I won't.' Rose looked important. She had been thrilled when Georgia had taken a chance on her and given her the job, and was even more pleased to find herself included in all the workings of the newspaper after being made to feel useless by her ex-husband for so long. 'Have a good evening. Are you meeting your friend?'

'My friend?'

'Mr Henderson. He *said* he knew you,' said Rose, suddenly anxious. She had made so many mistakes since she started, and she knew Georgia got impatient sometimes.

'Oh…Mac,' said Georgia. 'Yes, we did know each other a long time ago.'

'He seemed so nice,' said Rose. 'I thought he was absolutely charming.' Her voice dropped as she leant forward to whisper confidentially, 'And *very* attractive!'

Georgia couldn't help smiling at her tone. In spite of the disastrous end to her own marriage, Rose was very concerned about her boss's single state. She thought Georgia needed help bringing up Toby.

Georgia thought so too.

But Mac wasn't the man to help her. Toby needed a father figure, someone kind and steady like Geoffrey, not someone like Mac, who had never really grown up himself.

Toby, come and pick up some of these toys, please!'

Georgia sighed as she stooped to retrieve a sock from the living room floor. It had been a shock to realise just how much mess one small boy could generate.

She had thought no one could be messier than Mac, whose habit of carelessly discarding clothes wherever he happened to take them off had driven her mad when they were married, but Toby was even worse. His bedroom floor was carpeted with cards, small plastic figures, bits of paper, crayons, books, unidentified and probably broken pieces of toys, and a good deal else that Georgia preferred not to think about too closely.

Picking up a ball of what looked suspiciously like discarded chewing gum, she grimaced in disgust.

'Toby!' Her voice went up in spite of herself. She tried so hard to be patient and loving, but after a long day at work, with only a few minutes to prepare dinner for Geoffrey, let alone think about how she was going to deal with her soon-to-be ex-husband, it was a huge effort not to snap.

'There's someone coming to the door,' said Toby, which at least proved that he wasn't deaf. Ever anxious for an excuse to avoid tidying up, he was peering out of the window at the front of the house. He was wearing pyjamas and, having ignored her request to use a comb, his damp hair stuck out spikily in different directions.

'It'll just be someone delivering junk mail, I expect,' said Georgia, forcing herself to stay calm. Nothing was gained by losing her temper. Toby just withdrew even further into his shell.

'He's got a cool motorbike,' Toby commented, without leaving his vantage point at the window.

Georgia frowned slightly. Junk mail wasn't usually delivered by motorbike. Miss Sibley at number twenty-three often pushed newsletters for the local neighbourhood watch through the door at this sort of time, but she didn't ride a motorbike and, if she did, it certainly wouldn't be one Toby would describe as cool.

Curious, she went over to join Toby at the window. Sure enough, a motorbike was propped on its stand in the road outside the gate. It was a mean-looking machine, black and gleaming and very powerful, and something stirred inside Georgia. She knew only one person likely to ride a bike like that.

A sense of foreboding gripped her as the owner of the bike, hidden by the porch, rang the doorbell, and her frown deepened with suspicion. There was something awfully familiar about the arrogance of that ring.

'Who is it?' asked Toby.

Nobody could call Toby a beautiful child. He was thin and gap-toothed, with big ears and an expression that was usually sullen, but when he looked up at her, like now, with implicit trust that she would know the answer to everything, Georgia would feel her heart constrict.

'I don't know who it is,' she told him. *But I've*

got a pretty good idea, she added mentally. 'We'd better go and see.'

He followed her out into the hall and lurked behind her as she opened the door. Sure enough, there stood Mac, in faded jeans, a white T-shirt and his battered old leather jacket, camera slung as always around his neck. Not to put too fine a point on it, he looked gorgeous. His dark hair was ruffled where he had pulled off his helmet, and his blue eyes were warm with a smile that Georgia had to physically steel herself to resist.

'You're early,' she said brusquely. 'I said eight o'clock, and it's not even seven-thirty yet.'

'I thought it would be nice to meet Toby before he went to bed,' said Mac, completely unfazed by the hostile welcome, and he winked at Toby who was watching him with a wary expression.

'Who are you?' asked Toby, which seemed a fair enough question.

'This is Mac,' said Georgia quickly as Mac opened his mouth to answer. Life was complicated enough for Toby without trying to fathom his aunt's exact marital status. There was no need for him to know that she and Mac had been married.

Were still married, fool that she was. Why on earth hadn't she followed through with the divorce when they had first separated?

'I knew him a long time ago,' she said to Toby, trying to keep her explanation of this strange man's arrival as simple as possible. 'It was a real surprise when he turned up in Askerby, so I thought it would be nice if he came to dinner.'

Georgia had a nasty feeling that she was babbling, but Mac's presence on the doorstep was ridiculously disturbing.

He didn't look disturbed, of course. He looked utterly at ease, as always, with that good-humoured assurance that had taken him through more dangerous situations than Georgia cared to think about.

'Hi, Toby,' he said casually, but wisely made no move to get any closer or to engage him in conversation.

Toby was very wary of strangers and hated being overwhelmed by attention. It had taken him a long time to accept Georgia, and even now she still had to handle him with care. Geoffrey's laborious attempts at conversation were met with monosyllables at most. More worryingly, he didn't seem to be any more forthcoming at school, and he was slow to make friends.

Mac turned back to Georgia and produced a mango from his pocket with a flourish. 'For you,' he said, holding it in his outstretched palm, and Georgia's breath snared in her throat.

It was just a fruit. A beautiful piece of fruit, plump and juicy, its skin blushing from pinkish-green to ripe red, but still just a fruit, and not even that rare. You could even buy mangoes in Askerby nowadays, if you were lucky.

But for Georgia mangoes meant so much more than a exotic edge to a fruit salad. Mangoes meant long, hot tropical nights, creaking ceiling fans and eerie yips and yowls in the darkness beyond the veranda. Mangoes meant Mac. She had never eaten one until he had cut one carefully into almost-cubes so that she could bend back the skin and eat the fragrant orange flesh easily, and for her the taste would forever be associated with him. Just the sight of one was enough to swamp her with memories.

Almost without thinking, she reached out and took the mango from Mac and held it to her nose. Breathing in its distinctive smell, she was instantly transported back to their veranda in West Africa. Mac would cut up the mango for her and watch her as she ate it, the juice running down her chin.

'You eat mangoes the way you make love,' he would tell her, smiling in a way that made her blood flare, and he would lean across to kiss the stickiness away. 'I love the way you do that. Everyone else sees just a little bit of you, the particular, precise Georgia, but I know what you're really like. *I* know that behind that prim and proper façade, you're a very naughty girl!'

They always ended up making love when he brought her a mango.

It was the happiest Georgia had ever been. Memories of those times gripped her cruelly now, tightening her chest until she could hardly breathe. She could just stand there dumbly holding the mango, struggling to make her lungs work once more.

Why couldn't Mac be like Geoffrey, who brought her flowers without fail? They were always lovely flowers, not just a tired old bouquet from a garage forecourt, but nonetheless Georgia never had the sense that Geoffrey had any idea of what she would really like. He brought her flowers because that was the correct thing to do, and Geoffrey was always correct. Sometimes she wished he would surprise her, bring her a shiny conker he had picked up in the street, or a pot of honey, or a book that he thought she would enjoy.

Or a mango.

Why did Mac have to be different? she wondered in despair. Why did he have to choose the one gift that would mean so much, that would unlock so many memories? He had an uncanny ability to get under her skin when she least expected it, when she was certain that she could resist him, when she thought she was prepared.

Georgia's hands closed around the mango. 'You'd better come in,' she said, her voice shaking with the effort to keep it neutral.

'What's that?' said Toby as she stepped back to let Mac inside.

'This? It's a mango.'

'No, *that*,' he said impatiently, pointing at the camera around Mac's neck.

'It's my camera,' said Mac easily, and pulled it from around his neck. 'Do you want to have a look at it?'

Toby nodded and, to Georgia's consternation, Mac handed him the camera.

'Um...do you think that's a good idea?' she said meaningfully. The camera was his livelihood, after all, and professional cameras didn't come cheap.

'It's fine,' said Mac, looping the strap around Toby's neck. 'He won't drop it.'

Toby frowned down at the camera. 'It doesn't look like a camera,' he said suspiciously. 'It's not digital.'

'No,' Mac agreed solemnly, 'and you can't use it to make a phone call, either! This is a camera that just takes pictures.' He paused. 'Would you like me to show you how it works?'

Toby nodded again, and Georgia was too pleased to see him interested to object when Mac sat down with him on the sofa and showed him how to look through the camera and use the telescopic lens.

So much for clearing up before her visitors arrived. Mac wouldn't have noticed if he'd had to wade knee-deep through a rubbish tip to get to the sofa. He was as oblivious as Toby to any mess.

Life must be so much easier if you could just blank out whatever you didn't want to see, Georgia reflected. She would have loved to have been the kind of person who simply didn't notice or didn't care about her surroundings. Sadly, she was obsessive—according to Mac, anyway— about keeping her surroundings clean and tidy, and there was no way she could enjoy her supper with the room looking like this.

Sighing inwardly, Georgia got down on her knees and began to pick up toys while Mac and Toby bent their heads over the camera. She was too used to Mac continually clicking away to be bothered when they began pointing the camera at her and talking about framing a picture. One thing about being married to a photographer, you never got shy when someone got out their Instamatic and started snapping photos. After a while, it was just background noise and you stopped feeling self-conscious in front of a camera.

It was oddly comfortable to be clearing up while the man and the boy sat on the sofa, absorbed in what they were doing. It felt almost *normal*. Was this what it would have been like if she and Mac had had a family? Georgia wondered.

Wrapped up in her thoughts, she didn't at first register that Mac was talking to her.

'Sorry?' she said, sitting back on her haunches and smoothing a stray hair back from her face.

'I was just saying that Toby and I could finish tidying up if you want to go and change.'

Mac's blue eyes held a strange expression as they rested on her, and for some reason Georgia flushed.

'It's all right, thanks,' she said stiffly, aware for the first time that she was still wearing her work clothes. 'I don't usually bother to change any more.'

Mac frowned. He had always loved the moment when she would change in the evenings. That was when she would unbutton the crisp, cool Georgia and let the secret Georgia out, the Georgia who ate mangoes in a way that made the breath dry in his throat, the Georgia who was warm and loving and so sensuous that it was hard for him to think clearly when she was near.

'Why not?'

Georgia shrugged. 'Oh, the usual reason—no time. There's just too much to do every evening.'

And there was no one to change for any more, she added to herself as she gathered up some plastic counters that were scattered over the carpet.

Oh, there was Geoffrey, of course, but he inevitably came from work in his suit and, anyway, he would no doubt think that it was practical of her to stay in her work outfit too. Georgia couldn't imagine how he would react if she were to greet him at the door wearing one of the little numbers she had used to wear for Mac.

But she had been younger then, and everything was different now.

Mac watched her crouching down, piling Toby's toys into a box, and he felt the old familiar tightening of his chest. Her skirt was tight over her bottom and thighs, and he could see the graceful curve of her spine, the way her silky top rode up slightly as she stretched out.

He had once asked her why she wore such prim clothes instead of dressing like the warm, sexy woman that she really was. 'Because when I'm with you it's the only way I can keep any control over what's happening,' she had said. 'With you, everything's chaos. I don't know which way up I am when you're there, and when you're not I don't know where you are or what you're doing. At least if I get up and put on some suitable clothes to go to work, then I feel as if I've got some control over what's happening.'

Poor Georgia; it hadn't been easy for her, Mac thought with some compunction. She liked everything in its place and firmly under control, and she had never got used to the fact that love just didn't work like that.

'Can I take a picture of Georgia?' Toby asked him, holding the camera reverently.

'Sure,' said Mac absently, still thinking about Georgia.

'Look at me, Georgia!'

Glad to hear him sounding so animated, Georgia looked up dutifully and smiled.

Toby lifted the heavy camera in his thin hands and pointed it at her, then glanced up at Mac. 'Now?'

'Well, you *could* take it now,' Mac agreed, 'but she doesn't really look like Georgia when she's posing like that, does she? The thing about Georgia is that she's not an easy person to capture,' he went on easily, talking to Toby as if he were an interested adult rather than a small boy who simply wanted to press a button. 'You've got to think of it like hunting a wild animal. You have to be very quiet and wait until she's forgotten that you're there with a camera, and then—snap!— you can catch her unawares.'

Toby was listening intently to his advice, although Georgia was sure that he had no idea what Mac was talking about. She did, though. Catching her unawares, the way he had done today, was what Mac had always done best.

Well, he wasn't going to capture her this time.

Over Toby's head, she met Mac's amused navy-blue gaze, her own eyes bright with unspoken challenge, and the space between them was suddenly charged with an electric tension that sparked and sizzled alarmingly.

It was interrupted by the ring of the doorbell. 'That'll be Geoffrey.' Georgia leapt to her feet in relief. 'Toby, can you just finish putting away the last of the toys?' she asked, without much hope that he would oblige.

Toby heaved a sigh. 'Geoffrey's Georgia's boyfriend,' she heard him mutter glumly to Mac as she headed for the door. 'He's boring.'

Georgia suppressed an equally heavy sigh. She wished Toby would accept Geoffrey. He might not be fun or have a ridiculously expensive camera for Toby to fiddle with, but he was a nice man and very kind, quite apart from being the only friend they had at the moment.

She wished he wasn't standing on the other side of the door, though.

It was bad enough with Mac here, making her feel edgy and hassled, without having to deal with the two of them together. Dinner was shaping up to be its usual disaster, too. What Georgia really wanted was for both of them to disappear so that she could put Toby to bed and collapse on to the sofa with a stiff gin.

Still, it was too late for that now. Pinning a suitably bright smile to her face, she opened the front door.

CHAPTER THREE

PUNCTUAL to the minute, Geoffrey was standing there with—surprise, surprise—a bunch of flowers.

'They're lovely, thank you, Geoffrey,' said Georgia, dutifully accepting the proffered tulips and a kiss on the cheek. 'Come in.'

He followed her into the living room where, much to her surprise, Mac and Toby were on their knees, putting the last of the toys into the box.

'Oh...thank you,' she said, rather thrown by this evidence of helpfulness on Mac's part. She was fairly sure Toby wouldn't have done it on his own, but then Mac had never been able to comprehend the need to see the carpet before you walked on it, either.

'I knew you wouldn't relax until it was done,' said Mac virtuously. Getting to his feet in a leisurely way, he offered his hand to Geoffrey, who had stopped dead at the sight of him. 'Hello, there,' he said.

Too late, Georgia realised that she should have thought how she was going to handle the introductions. 'Um…you remember Mac, don't you, Geoffrey?'

'Mac…?' Geoffrey looked at her in dawning dismay.

'Mac Henderson,' Mac reminded him helpfully, and quite unnecessarily. 'Georgia's husband.'

'*Ex*-husband,' snapped Georgia.

'*Husband*?' said Toby.

'We met once at dinner at Georgia's parents' house,' Mac went on, obviously enjoying Geoffrey's consternation.

'I remember,' said Geoffrey stiffly, taking Mac's hand and shaking it with obvious reluctance.

'Husband?' Toby asked again, looking from Georgia to Mac. 'Does that mean you're married?'

'No,' said Georgia, just as Mac said 'Yes,' and Geoffrey looked disapproving.

Georgia sucked in her breath crossly, furious with Mac for mentioning the subject in the first place, but reluctant to start an argument in front of Toby.

'It's a long story,' she told him after a moment. 'I'll explain it to you later, but for now I think it's time for bed.'

Toby's mouth turned down at the corners. 'But it's not time yet!' he said with a scowl.

'It *is* time,' Georgia insisted. The prickly atmosphere was making her edgy, and gave her voice a sharper edge than normal.

'Oh, but *Georgia*...' Toby moaned. 'Mac hasn't finished showing me his camera.'

'I can do that upstairs.' Mac stepped in, seeing that Georgia was looking frazzled. 'Why don't you show me your room, and we can take a picture up there? I expect Georgia would like to talk to Geoffrey on her own, anyway.'

Georgia would, but she didn't like Mac calmly arranging her life for her. On the other hand, getting Toby upstairs was half the battle most of the time, and she didn't want to embark on a big confrontation in front of Geoffrey, who thought Toby was too undisciplined at the best of times.

'That's a good idea,' she said, managing a tight smile. 'Why don't you go up with Mac, and I'll come up and say goodnight in a bit?'

'What's *he* doing here?' Geoffrey demanded the moment they had gone.

'He says he wants to talk about the divorce,' said Georgia, conscious of a twinge of irritation.

She didn't have to explain to Geoffrey. She'd made it very clear that for now they were simply friends, and that she wasn't prepared to take their relationship any further until she had divorced Mac. She had every intention of doing that, but until then Geoffrey had no right to disapprove of anyone she chose to invite to her home.

'He turned up out of the blue this afternoon,

and I thought it would be better to talk about things over supper. There's no reason we shouldn't be civilized about this.'

'You might have warned me!' said Geoffrey, still huffy.

'I tried, but Ruth said that you were busy.'

'I was with a client, hence I couldn't come to the phone.'

Irritation flickered again at Geoffrey's fondness for the word 'hence'. He used it a lot and it always grated on Georgia, although she wasn't usually as exasperated by it as she was today.

That was Mac's fault, she thought darkly. Geoffrey had hardly irritated her at all until he turned up. He had just been kind and helpful and friendly—as he still was, Georgia reminded herself guiltily. She could put up with 'hence' if it meant having a steady, reliable friend like Geoffrey by her side.

'I'm sorry,' she said penitently. 'I wish I had been able to warn you that Mac would be here tonight. It was a bit of a shock to me too when he turned up, but perhaps it's not a bad thing. Now that he's here we can talk properly, face to face, and sort things out. With any luck Mac will sign the papers while he's here, and then I'll be able to move on. I did explain that I didn't want to start a proper relationship with you until I'd done that.'

'Yes, you did,' Geoffrey agreed. 'And you

know I think you're worth waiting for. I've waited a long time, and I don't mind waiting a bit longer.' He smiled. 'But you can't blame me for getting impatient sometimes!'

Georgia kissed him impulsively on the cheek. 'Thanks for understanding, Geoffrey.'

How different he was to Mac, who would never have stood patiently by and given her the space she needed to sort out another relationship! With Mac it was always all or nothing.

Which only went to show that Geoffrey was a much better man for her.

Geoffrey followed her into the kitchen as she checked the meal. She had never been a very enthusiastic cook—OK, she was a terrible cook—but Geoffrey liked home cooking, so she was trying to make more of an effort.

After all, he was making so much more of an effort for her. He was holding back when he could have been pushing, giving her time when he could have been issuing ultimatums, offering support when she needed it most. Trying to follow a few recipes seemed the least she could do in return, although there were times, like now, when she was tired after a day at work and dealing with Toby, that Georgia wished she could just pop into the supermarket on the way home and buy something easy.

Tonight she was making pork with prunes followed by plum crumble. Geoffrey wasn't fond of garlic or spices, which made it difficult to come up with ideas sometimes, but this menu had seemed safe enough. Shame it was all so…brown.

Georgia wrinkled her nose and closed the oven door. Too late to do anything about it now. She would just have to hope that it tasted better than it looked.

Leaving Geoffrey in charge of opening a bottle of wine, she went upstairs to say goodnight to Toby. Rather to her surprise, she found him sitting up in bed and chatting to Mac.

She paused, unnoticed, in the doorway, struck by the animation in Toby's face. He never looked that happy and interested when he was with her, she thought sadly, and her eyes slid of their own accord over to Mac, who was lounging on the other bed, arms behind his head and long legs crossed, careless of his boots on the coverlet, and looking utterly relaxed.

He looked up just then and caught sight of her. 'Uh-oh,' he said to Toby. 'Looks like your time's up!'

'I'm in bed,' Toby declared, somewhat unnecessarily.

'So I see,' said Georgia, coming into the room and trying not to notice how inviting the space on the bed next to Mac looked. 'Good boy!'

'Mac said I should. He said it would be…what was that word again, Mac?'

'Politic,' said Mac with a grin.

'... he said it would be *politic* if I was in bed before you came up,' Toby finished guilelessly.

Georgia suppressed a smile at the earnestness in his face as she sat on the edge of his bed. 'Did he explain what that meant?'

Toby screwed up his face in an effort of memory. 'That it would make life easier for me if I did what you wanted?'

'Sounds like good advice to me,' she agreed, and glanced at Mac, who had swung his legs on to the floor and was watching her, amusement glinting in his navy blue eyes. 'It's made life easier for both of us.'

'Maybe you should take my advice more often,' said Mac with mock smugness.

'Oh, you're an expert on childcare now, are you?' said Georgia, keeping her tone light in front of Toby.

'I'm an expert in making life as easy and as comfortable as you can make it under the circumstances,' said Mac. 'It's called making the best of things.'

Yes, he'd always been good at that, thought Georgia. He was good at living for the moment, at living each day as if it might be his last. He didn't do worrying and planning the way she did. He didn't agonize about what people thought, or waste any time feeling torn between conflicting demands.

He would have made a lousy woman.

Georgia turned back to Toby and tweaked his nose affectionately. '*You* might as well make the best of things now and go to sleep. You've got school in the morning.'

'I'm not tired,' said Toby automatically. It was a point of honour never to admit that he was tired, but he seemed quite happy tonight to snuggle down under his duvet.

'Goodnight, Toby,' said Mac, reaching down to ruffle his hair gently, and Georgia had to close her eyes for a moment against the tantalising effect of his nearness.

It was a relief when Mac moved away. Leaning forward, she kissed Toby gently on the cheek. He didn't kiss her back, but it was a big step even to get this far, and Georgia was always very careful not to push it.

'Sleep well,' she said.

Mac watched her from the doorway, touched by the combination of tenderness and awkwardness she showed with Toby, and shaken by a contrasting memory of Georgia sitting on the edge of the bed, smiling as she leant forward to kiss *him*. She acted so cool, but her lips had been so soft, her body so warm.

It came to something when you were jealous of a small boy, he reflected wryly. Then he thought of Geoffrey and his expression hardened. Did Geoffrey know what it was like to be kissed by Georgia?

It wasn't a thought that Mac liked. He didn't like it at all.

And he didn't like the way Geoffrey offered him a glass of wine when he went downstairs, playing mine host while Georgia was in the kitchen, and making polite conversation for all the world as if he belonged here with Georgia and Mac was a mere visitor in their house.

It turned out that Georgia had taken to cooking, too. Mac had always teased her about her incompetence in the kitchen, rather liking the fact that here was one area in which the practical Georgia fell far short of her own perfectionist standards. She just didn't seem to have a feel for food at all. He himself was quite happy to cook when he had the time, but they had lived off takeaways and ready made meals for a large part of their married life.

But now it seemed that Georgia was lashed to the stove every night after work and struggling through recipes. Mac didn't mind her making the effort. Knowing how much she hated cooking, he even admired her for it. What he *did* mind was the fact that she appeared to be doing it for Geoffrey, who had gourmet pretensions and disapproved of fast food and prepared meals.

'They're full of salt and additives,' he explained to Mac.

Worst of all, from Mac's point of view anyway, Georgia had even attempted to make Geoffrey a plum crumble, allegedly his favourite pudding, although it had to be said that it wasn't a success. The supposed crisp topping had sunk into the fruit that was swimming in juice and created an unappetising brown sludge.

Geoffrey waded through his bowl and pronounced it delicious.

Mac caught Georgia's eye. 'I should stick to ordering takeaways if I were you,' he said in a stage whisper and she laughed reluctantly.

'I just don't seem to be able to get the hang of cooking.'

'Oh, come now, you've improved a lot,' said Geoffrey.

It might have been meant kindly, but it came over as deeply patronising in Mac's book, and he eyed the other man with acute dislike. What on earth did Georgia see in him? He was fair and dependable-looking, with regular features, and might even be considered handsome in a pale, wishy-washy kind of way, if you liked that kind of thing, but Mac thought him pompous and dull.

Still, there was no doubt that he was loyal to Georgia. He was bristling now at Mac's implied criticism.

'I think she's marvellous,' Geoffrey said. 'And she hasn't changed a bit since I first knew her, which is a very long time now, I can tell you! She's just as beautiful now as she was then!'

This was clearly designed to impress on Mac

Geoffrey's prior claim on Georgia. Profoundly unimpressed, Mac glanced at Georgia, who was squirming slightly. She hated effusive compliments, in public at least. She was a strictly behind-closed-doors kind of woman. If Geoffrey knew her as intimately as he wanted to suggest, he would have known that.

Mac sat back in his chair. 'Ah, yes, you two were childhood sweethearts, weren't you?'

'We weren't sweethearts,' admitted Geoffrey with a touch of regret. 'Just friends.'

'Didn't you used to do your Latin homework together or something?'

'That's right.' Geoffrey looked misty-eyed at the memory, but Georgia shifted uncomfortably.

'They must have been happy days. All that declining of verbs, eh?' Mac shook his head in mock envy. 'Practising those conjugations, working out your ablative from your genitive...pretty hot stuff!'

He was making fun of them, thought Georgia crossly If only she and Geoffrey had a wild and wacky history together, smoking pot behind the bike sheds or skiving off school to go and see a band with an aggressive or unfathomable name. Somehow the two school swots doing their homework together didn't make for many very exciting memories!

'It was very useful,' Geoffrey told him. 'We both got an A.'

'More crumble, Geoffrey?' Georgia interposed quickly, before Mac could get in with some caustic comment that would make Geoffrey look ridiculous.

It was obvious that the two men disliked each other, and she was beginning to feel exhausted with the strain of averting a full-scale confrontation. Anxious to steer the conversation into more neutral waters, she turned to Geoffrey and asked him about his day.

It wasn't a very interesting or inspiring topic, but Geoffrey seemed happy to talk, and as long as he did that she could concentrate on him and not on Mac who was listening with a derisive expression. At least she could try.

It was a huge effort to keep her head tilted at an interested angle and her body turned towards Geoffrey when every nerve was straining to swing round, like a needle finding north, to where Mac sat, dark and disturbing, on her other side. She could feel his eyes on her, making her skin tingle and quiver with awareness, while she fought desperately to follow what Geoffrey was saying.

It wasn't anything worth listening to, in Mac's opinion. As far as he could make out, Geoffrey was pontificating to Georgia about holidays. 'You can't beat the Med if you want two weeks away from it all,' Geoffrey was claiming, and instead of laughing and saying of *course* you could beat the Mediterranean, there were loads of interesting and exotic countries in the world, Georgia just nodded encouragingly.

Mac couldn't believe it. Rather surprisingly for someone so immaculately groomed, Georgia had always loved wild country. It didn't matter if it were the Sahara or the Serengeti, the more remote the place, the wider the horizon, the brighter her eyes shone. She was relaxed about insects, and never fussed about comfort or cleanliness or being made to walk for hours under the burning sun.

His heart ached as he remembered making love to her under the stars. Where had that Georgia gone? The Georgia who had dreamt of walking the Inca trail in Peru and watching the sun rise over Macchu Pichu was apparently now content to spend her holidays in a Mediterranean resort with full plumbing and catering facilities!

Look at her, listening so intently to Geoffrey. Anyone would think that she was fascinated by the way she kept her eyes fixed on Geoffrey's face, Mac thought sourly, and whenever the other man seemed to be winding down, she would murmur something encouraging to set him off again.

Mac himself had given up even the pretence of listening. With Georgia's attention so firmly fixed on Geoffrey, he could allow himself the luxury of simply looking at her. He searched her face, trying to find tiny differences, comparing her now with the way he remembered her so vividly in his dreams.

She was older, of course, but in some indefinable way she seemed to have grown into her looks. Her skin might have lost the freshness and glow of youth, and there were telltale lines edging her eyes, but she still had the beautiful bone structure that gave her face its character and the silky hair was untouched by any grey, at least that he could see. Maybe her hairdresser knew better.

Mac's eyes rested on the curve of her jaw for a while before drifting down her throat to the fine line of her clavicle revealed by the scoop-necked top, and all at once he was gripped by the need to touch her, to hold her, to feel her skin beneath his hands once more. How had he lasted four years without her? God, he wished that Geoffrey would go.

'Mac? Are you all right?'

Mac jerked back to attention to realise that they were both looking at him, Georgia with concern mixed with curiosity, and Geoffrey with hostility. Perhaps he had been able to read Mac's expression more easily than Georgia had.

'Yes, I'm fine,' said Mac, recovering quickly. 'I was just thinking what a great house this was.' It was a poor reason for staring at Georgia's cleavage, but it would have to do.

And actually, it *was* a nice house when he looked round at it. The floor was stripped pine and the décor simple and, although there wasn't very much furniture, the few pieces that there were looked comfortable and well-designed. The open plan living room made it feel light and airy, and yet there was a warmth to the decoration too. It was a restful, uncluttered room, not unlike Georgia herself.

And a complete contrast to the messy studio he used as a base in London. That was just somewhere to sleep and store his stuff. It wasn't a home.

Come to think of it, there hadn't been anywhere to call home since he and Georgia had separated.

'Was it like this when you bought it?' he went on, thinking that it was time that he contributed something to the conversation. It was sad when you had to talk to your own wife about property, but it was better than listening to Geoffrey droning on.

'No, I had to get rid of a lot of stuff when I moved in,' Georgia told him. She seemed glad of the neutral topic. 'Do you remember those horrible carpets?' she added to Geoffrey, turning her mouth down at the very memory of them.

She turned back to Mac. 'Geoffrey was fantastic when I moved in. He put up shelves and pictures and took all the old stuff to the dump and fixed dripping taps and helped move furniture around…I don't know what I'd have done without him!'

Mac scowled. He didn't want to hear what a great help Geoffrey had been. He'd obviously been round every evening with his screwdriver and his drill, making himself indispensable. *He* would have been able to do all that for Georgia too.

But he hadn't been there, had he?

Looking across the table, he could read the unmistakable satisfaction in Geoffrey's eyes. It was clear that the other man was thinking exactly the same thing.

Mac's expression hardened. So Geoffrey wasn't above taking advantage of Georgia's gratitude. Perhaps he would be harder to see off than Mac had anticipated, but then, Mac had never been one to resist a challenge. He certainly wasn't about to give up tamely just because Geoffrey could put up a few shelves.

'It looks like you've made yourself at home, anyway,' he said, turning back to Georgia. 'Does that mean you're planning on staying here?'

What he really wanted to know was whether she was planning on moving in with Geoffrey.

'As long as Toby's at school,' said Georgia, assuming that Mac was talking about Askerby rather than the house itself. 'It really depends on whether I can turn the paper around.'

'Is that what you were brought in to do?'

Faint colour touched Georgia's cheekbones. 'I wasn't exactly brought in,' she confessed. 'The *Gazette* was bought about a year ago by Griff Carver—you might have heard of him?'

'I have,' said Mac, pursing his lips in a silent whistle. 'He's worth serious money. Isn't he the original bad boy makes good?'

'I don't know about making good, but he's certainly made a lot of money,' said Georgia dryly.

'Most of it by very dubious methods, from what I hear,' Geoffrey added disapprovingly. 'He's from Askerby, and a lot of people remember him when he was just the local troublemaker. It didn't go down well when he bought the *Gazette*.'

This was beginning to sound interesting, thought Mac. 'So what's your connection with Carver?' he asked Georgia, who was looking slightly uncomfortable. He sensed that her relationship with Griff Carver, whatever it was, hadn't gone down very well with Geoffrey either.

'I wanted to bring Toby back to Askerby, and my only chance of a job where I could use my experience as a journalist was on the *Gazette*. I knew it had just been sold, so I went to see Griff Carver and told him what he already knew: that the paper was on its knees, that circulation had been dropping for years and that unless he brought in someone to revitalise the content and the writing, it would fold.'

'It wouldn't matter that much to him, though, would it? The *Gazette* can only be a tiny part of his business. If it folded, he'd just write it off as a tax loss.'

'Maybe, but I had the feeling that Griff Carver doesn't like to be associated with failure.'

'So you offered yourself as the editor who could turn the *Gazette* round?' Mac sat back in his chair and regarded Georgia with admiration.

'More or less,' she said, toying with the stem of her wineglass. 'I told him I could make the *Askerby and District Gazette* an exciting, innovative paper that would transform the image of local journalism.'

'And he bought that?'

Georgia thought back to that interview with Griff Carver. 'I think he was intrigued by the idea of showing all his detractors that he could make a success of the paper, in spite of local opinion, but he's not exactly the sentimental type. He's not going to throw good money after bad, if I can't make a success of it…' She trailed off with an eloquent shrug. 'The fact is that things haven't got off to a good start.'

Which had to be the understatement of the year.

'Meeting with resistance, are you?'

'Just a bit,' said Georgia, a bitter edge to her voice. 'I didn't count on how much resistance there would be to change, and it didn't help that Griff didn't even consult the former editor. He just sacked him and announced that I would be taking over, with the result that the reporter, the photographer, the accountant and the editor's secretary all walked out in protest.'

She sighed at the memory of those chaotic months. 'I spent the first few weeks trying to hold things together while I found new staff, but the only people who'd work with me are new to the job, and I still haven't found a photographer.'

'Ah...hence your interviews this afternoon?'

'That's right.' Georgia sighed. 'What a waste of time *they* were! Amateurs, every one of them.'

She shook her head. 'I don't know what I'm going to do. The professionals around here are making much more money doing weddings and portraits, and anyone interested in being a news photographer certainly isn't interested in Askerby.'

'Who's taking pictures at the moment?'

'We've got Gary, who at least seems to know one end of a camera from another, but he's only just finished a photography course at the local college. He really needs to work with someone who knows what they're doing so that he can get some training, but judging by the interviews there's no one in Askerby who knows more than he does.'

'Perhaps I'll apply for the job,' said Mac casually.

Georgia wasn't about to fall for that one. 'Yeah, right. Award-winning photographer Mackenzie Henderson gives up covering international conflicts in favour of the *Askerby and District Gazette*.'

Mac smiled. 'Maybe I feel like a change.'

Yes, and maybe swarms of winged pigs were grunting their way over the rooftops of Askerby as they spoke!

'Well, if you're that keen, we'd certainly be prepared to take you on for a month—on a trial basis, of course!' said Georgia, without bothering to conceal her sarcasm. 'There's an editorial conference tomorrow at ten. Perhaps you could come along and meet your future colleagues then?'

'OK,' said Mac with a grin.

Georgia thought the joke had gone on long enough, and anyway the very mention of photographers had reminded her of her most pressing problem.

'But, seriously, I must be able to find a photographer *somewhere*.' She sighed, forgetting Mac for a moment. 'I'll just have to advertise further afield, I suppose. I wish I could sort something out. I can't make any real changes at the paper unless I've got someone to take some decent pictures...'

There was a tiny crease between her brows, and her bottom lip was caught beneath her teeth. Mac had often seen her ponder a problem with just such an intent expression and he was gripped by a sudden strange mixture of affection and lust.

He wanted to pull her on to his lap, to kiss the crease from her brow and make her smile and solve her problem for her. He wanted to make everything all right for her, and then he wanted to take her to bed and make love to her until she forgot that she had ever had a problem in the first place.

But, before he could give in to the impulse to reach for her, Georgia had shaken herself with a visible effort and was pushing back her chair.

'I'll put the kettle on.'

'No coffee for me, thanks, Georgia,' said Geoffrey, hoisting himself to his feet. 'I must be going.'

'But it's still early,' she protested in dismay.

They still hadn't talked about the divorce and she had counted on Geoffrey to be by her side while she faced Mac. Georgia didn't trust herself on her own. Ever since Mac had handed her that mango and smiled, she had been fighting the pull of memory and the dark, dangerous tug of attraction that still existed between them, however much she tried to deny it to herself.

As long as Geoffrey was there, she could be sensible and remember why she had written to Mac to finalise the long-postponed divorce.

But once he had gone...

'I've got an early meeting tomorrow,' Geoffrey was explaining. 'I want to get a good night's sleep so that I'm fresh for it.'

What could be so important about a meeting of chartered surveyors that necessitated an extra two hours' sleep? Georgia wondered resentfully, but she tried not to show her chagrin and went to the door with him, waiting while he buttoned up his coat.

It wasn't fair to blame Geoffrey for leaving her. He thought of her as a sensible woman who was perfectly capable of having a rational discussion about divorce with the husband from whom she had been separated for four years.

After all, Geoffrey would doubtless point out, it had been a mutual decision to separate, and there were no children to complicate the issue. The London house they had owned together had been sold four years ago, and the proceeds split down the middle, so there were no financial issues to settle either. What on earth could be the problem?

How could Geoffrey understand the shivery sensation that hummed under her skin whenever Mac was near, the pulse of her body, the beating of her blood? That old black magic. Ella Fitzgerald had known what she was singing about.

But she didn't have to give in to it, and she wouldn't. She *was* a sensible woman. She could acknowledge the sexual chemistry between her and Mac, but it hadn't been enough to keep their marriage going before, and it wouldn't now. She just had to remember that.

Still, when Geoffrey kissed her decorously on the cheek and thanked her for dinner, punctiliously polite as always, she had to resist the urge to cling to him and beg him not to go and leave her alone with Mac.

'I'll ring you tomorrow,' said Geoffrey, oblivious to her tension, and headed off into the night.

Abandoning her.

Georgia closed the door on the cold and took a breath. There was no point in dithering out here in the hall. It wasn't as if she was afraid of Mac.

Just of the way he made her feel.

Hugging her arms around her in an unconsciously defensive posture, she went back into the living room, where Mac was helping himself to more crumble. He looked up at her with one of those grins that set her nerves jitterbugging.

'You know, it doesn't taste as bad as it looks,' he said. 'Have some more.'

Georgia shuddered as she dropped back into her chair. 'I don't think I'll ever be able to face crumble again!'

'Oh, but it's Geoffrey's favourite,' Mac reminded her unfairly. 'And if it's not crumble, it'll be apple pie or jam roly-poly or treacle pudding. Geoffrey's a pudding kind of guy.'

It was true. Georgia looked across the table at him, leaning easily back in his chair. She knew how quickly he could snap into action when he wanted. It was very easy to underestimate Mac. Georgia had come to recognize that his apparently lazy grace masked a coiled strength. He reminded her of a big cat lolling in the shade, who could change in an instant into a dangerous hunter.

He wasn't a nursery pudding kind of guy. He wasn't a champagne and caviare man either. He was the kind of man who would eat from a bowl of fiery chillies, the kind of man you shared a whisky with while sheltering from the tropical rain, a man who bought you fresh mangoes and kissed away the juice that trickled down your chin...

Georgia swallowed. There was absolutely no point in going down that particular memory road.

'I'd better practise my baking then,' she said, but was unable to keep the weariness from her voice. 'I certainly can't make him any nice puddings at the moment.'

'You can't be good at everything, Georgia.' Mac's voice was unusually gentle. 'So you're not a domestic goddess? Who cares? You're a great journalist and a brilliant editor. Doesn't that mean more than being able to knock up an apple crumble? Stop trying to be superwoman.'

'I'm not trying to be anything,' said Georgia. 'Most of the time, my only ambition is to get through the day!'

'Then why do you care what your puddings look like?'

Georgia lifted her chin and met the navy blue gaze directly. 'Because Geoffrey cares,' she said deliberately.

CHAPTER FOUR

MAC didn't answer immediately. He swirled the last few drops of wine around in the bottom of his glass and contemplated them for a moment. When he lifted his eyes, his expression wasn't angry as Georgia expected, but almost compassionate.

'He's not the man for you, Georgia,' he said.

'He *is*.' Georgia wasn't sure whether she was trying to convince Mac or herself. 'He's kind and loyal and decent and patient.'

'And you've got virtually nothing in common with him, apart from Askerby.'

'Askerby is my life now. And it's Geoffrey's life. Maybe it's not very exciting or glamorous compared to Chad or Chile or wherever else you've been recently, but this is where I have to be now.'

'Life's too short to spend it somewhere you don't want to be, Georgia,' said Mac, shaking his head.

'Easy for you to say,' she said with an edge of

bitterness. 'You only have to think about yourself.'

Picking up her glass, Georgia realised that it was empty and sighed in frustration. 'Oh, God, let's have some more wine. I need it after the day I've had.'

She fetched a bottle of red from the kitchen but made such a hash of opening it that Mac took the corkscrew from her, removed the cork and refilled her glass, all without a word, while Georgia tried not to notice how deft his fingers were, how strong and competent and reassuring his hands looked.

'Thank you,' she said, tearing her eyes away and picking up her glass instead, glad of something to do with her own hands.

She sipped the wine as she tried to think of how to explain her position to Mac. She didn't want to fight about it. She was too tired for an argument. She would rather he understood why she wanted the divorce now. Surely then he would go away and leave her to settle back into the dull life she had chosen instead of stirring her up and unsettling her and making it hard to remember why she had made the choice she had.

'Look,' she said slowly, 'coming back to Askerby was never part of my plan. I had a good life in London. A nice flat, friends, a job I loved...I didn't want to give any of it up.'

It had been what had kept her going in the long,

bleak years after she had told Mac that if they wanted such different things out of their marriage it would be better to walk away before they tore each other apart. She had wanted to shock him into changing, into realising that they would both have to give up something if they wanted their relationship to survive.

Deep down, Georgia knew, she had wanted him to refuse, to insist that she was his wife and always would be, but Mac hadn't done that. He had agreed that they would only hurt each other if they stayed together, so they had gone their separate ways. Georgia had sold the house, sent him half the proceeds, and thrown herself into her career, and Mac had gone back to Africa.

Oh, and broken her heart.

If he wasn't prepared to make any effort to save their marriage, there was no point in her struggling by herself. Separating had been the right decision, Georgia still thought that, but she hadn't counted on how much it would hurt or how desperately she would miss him.

Having an absorbing and exciting job had saved her, and Georgia had clung on to it as long as she could.

'I should have come back to Askerby as soon as Becca died,' she said, shifting a little in her chair as she tried to shrug off the guilt that still lingered. 'Mum never wanted me to go in the first place, and I feel bad about not coming back for her, but I loved my job…'

She sighed, wishing there was a way she could undo the choices she had made.

'I was selfish, I guess.'

'There's nothing selfish about having a life and a career of your own,' said Mac, who had privately always thought that Georgia's mother, like her sister, was more than capable of looking after herself, and had simply found it easier to let Georgia do everything for them. 'There's no reason why you shouldn't still be in London.'

'I've got Toby to think about now,' she reminded him.

'So? Millions of children grow up perfectly happily in London.'

'Not Toby. He was miserable there, and it seemed to me that he'd had enough to cope with, losing his mother and his grandmother. He's not the easiest little boy at the best of times.'

She paused. 'Yes, I could have kept my high-powered job and stayed in London. I could have bought a house with a garden, although I wouldn't have been able to afford much of one, and I could have found an au pair or a nanny to look after him, but I didn't want Toby to grow up that way. Lots of single parents don't have a choice, but I did. All I had to do was find myself a job in Askerby.'

'So that's why you went to Griff Carver?'

'Yes.' Georgia flushed. 'I'm sorry the last editor lost his job because of me, but if he'd carried on, the paper would have folded by now and he'd have been out of a job anyway. And, frankly, I wasn't thinking about him. I was thinking about Toby. I owe it to Becca to bring him up the best way I can, and the best place for him is Askerby.'

'Ironic that you ended up giving up your precious career for a child after all, isn't it?' said Mac with a trace of bitterness, and she bit her lip.

'Yes, it is,' she agreed in a low voice, 'but these things happen. I didn't feel as if I had a choice when it came to Toby. I *did* have a choice about whether or not to have a family with you. And one thing having Toby has taught me, Mac, is that I made the right decision not to do that. It's hard, harder than you can possibly imagine, to bring up a child on your own.'

'But you wouldn't have been on your own if we'd had a family together,' he objected.

'Effectively I would have been,' said Georgia. 'I suppose I could have handed a baby over to a nanny and gone straight back to work, but what would have been the point in that? And even if I had been happy to do that, what would I have done if the baby had been ill? You wouldn't have been there.'

'Yes, I would!' he said hotly. 'I was the one who wanted a family, dammit!'

'Oh, I'm sure you would have *meant* to do your

share of the childcare, but how often would you have had to drop everything and jump on a plane at a couple of hours' notice? Who would have been left holding the baby then? You were always chasing pictures for the breaking story,' Georgia reminded him. 'You spend *months* in war zones sometimes. You wouldn't have been there for a child any more than you were there for me.'

Mac flinched. 'I would have done anything for you, Georgia.'

'Anything but compromise,' she said.

'What was I supposed to do, give up my job?' he said angrily.

'You were asking me to give up mine,' she pointed out. 'What made your career so much more important than mine?'

'It wasn't. It was just…what else could I have done?' Mac raked his hand through his hair in frustration. 'I'm a photographer!'

'You didn't have to be a photographer always on assignments overseas,' said Georgia. 'You could have settled down, applied for home assignments, but no! You were Mackenzie Henderson, hotshot war photographer. You weren't going to change anything about *your* life. It was all about what *I* had to give up, all about the compromises *I* would have to make while you weren't prepared to make any!'

She stopped, her voice shaking, as the old resentment flared, bringing back too many memories of other old, bitter arguments just like this.

There was an unpleasant silence.

Georgia looked away from Mac's grim face. What was the point of arguing? It was over. Surely that was what she needed to make him understand?

'Anyway,' she said heavily after moment, 'I've decided that Toby will be happier in Askerby, and that means that I have to be in Askerby too. I've stopped fighting it and accepted my fate. This is just the way things have to be now. Toby needs stability, and I need security.'

She paused. 'It's not the exciting, high-powered life I'd planned, but at least I've had a taste of that, and now I have to settle for what I've got. And, when you think about it, that's a lot. Toby's OK and I've got my own home and a job that may not be the one I dreamt of, but at least it's a challenge.'

'And where does Geoffrey fit into all this?' Mac couldn't keep the hostility out of his voice. 'Why do you need him too?'

Georgia put down her glass, hesitating as she tried to find the words to explain. 'I don't *need* anyone, but Geoffrey's made it clear that he's there if I want him. And, OK, it may not be a wild and passionate romance, but he's offering reliability, steadiness, friendship... Those things count for a lot. If I'm settling for a sensible life here, I may as well settle for a sensible relationship too.

'That's why I want this divorce, Mac,' she said, looking at him with direct grey eyes. 'I want to start again with a clean slate. I've tried passion and excitement and living on the edge,' she told him with a feeble attempt at a smile. 'You don't love like that twice in a lifetime, I know that, but I wasn't very good at it first time round, and now I want something different. I want security and…and *calm*. I don't want to *think* any more,' she said wearily. 'I'm tired of dealing with everything on my own. I'm tired, full stop. I want someone steady to be a good friend to me. Is that too much to ask?'

Mac's jaw hardened. 'And you think Geoffrey can do that for you?' he said, and the thread of contempt for the other man in his voice made Georgia's temper spurt.

'I know Geoffrey can be a bit stuffy sometimes,' she said, holding on to it with difficulty, 'but he's a nice man, a decent man, and he's attractive and single—and he wants me,' she added. 'He'll help me and support me and be a kind father figure to Toby.'

Mac shook his head. 'But he won't make you happy.'

The certainty in his voice grated on Georgia. Losing the battle with her temper, she shoved back her chair angrily and began stacking the pudding plates.

'Mac, you don't know me any more,' she said tightly. 'I've changed in the last four years.'

'Not that much.'

'What right have you got to waltz back into my life after all this time and start talking to me about happiness?' she demanded furiously, banging spoons into one of the bowls. 'You know nothing about me now, *nothing*! What makes you think you know what I need? Just because you find Geoffrey dull, that doesn't mean that I do!'

'I didn't say he was dull,' said Mac. 'Although he is. I'm saying that he doesn't seem to have a clue what you're really like, and I don't think you can be happy with someone who doesn't understand you.'

'The way you do, I suppose?'

Mac ignored her sarcasm. 'Yes, the way I do.'

'Geoffrey's known me a long time,' said Georgia, angrily slapping the top on the plastic pot of cream. Geoffrey would probably have liked it if she'd put it in a jug, but she hadn't thought. Mac was right, she was never going to make a domestic goddess. 'It's possible he knows me even better than you do.'

'He's still thinking of you as a nice schoolgirl, Georgia. You're the girl next door, the one he dreamt about, the one he sat down and conjugated Latin verbs with, but you're not that nice little

girl any more. I don't think Geoffrey has any idea
of where you've been, about what you've done,
what makes you laugh, what makes you cry… He
hasn't got a clue what you're really like.'

'And nor do you, Mac,' Georgia flared, grey
eyes blazing. She didn't look so cool now. 'Oh,
I know you think you do. I know that when everyone else saw me as that nice Georgia Maitland,
such a sensible, reliable girl, a bit prickly perhaps,
but clever and so capable, you saw a different side
to me. You taught me to enjoy my body, and you
showed me the world in a way I'd never seen it
before, and I'll always be grateful to you for that.'

Grateful?' A muscle beat furiously in Mac's
jaw. 'Is that what you think I want you to feel?'

Georgia closed her eyes briefly in frustration.
'Mac, I'm trying to tell you how I felt, how I still
feel…but you're not listening, are you? It's not
about *you* and how *you* want me to feel. This is
about *me*! If you're not interested, if you don't
want to know what went wrong in our marriage,
then I'll just shut up.'

After a visible effort to control his temper, Mac
unclenched his jaw. 'I *am* interested, and I'm listening. Go on, tell me.'

'All right.' Georgia had her own temper under
control once more. Forgetting that she was still
holding the pudding bowls, she thought about
how she could best make him understand.

'Those first few years with you were wonderful,' she began slowly. 'When we lived in Africa…I've never been happier. It was like we were discovering the world together.' She looked at him. 'You know how good things were between us then.'

When Mac nodded, she went on. 'When we came back to London, though, things seemed to change. It wasn't that I thought you didn't love me any more, but it was as if I was some kind of toy that you'd discovered and played with for a while, and had a good time teaching all you knew about love and happiness.

'And that was a lot, Mac,' said Georgia seriously. 'Nobody knows more about enjoying life than you do. It was such fun being married to you.'

'Then where did the fun go?' asked Mac, his expression bleak as he remembered all the good times they had shared.

'I don't know. That's what I'm trying to explain. Maybe we just got too familiar with each other. Maybe other things seemed more interesting and exciting than me after a while. That was how it seemed to me, anyway.'

Mac frowned then. 'I never lost interest in you!'

'It felt like that,' Georgia told him sadly. 'It felt as if you'd stopped looking at me properly, stopping seeing me for who I was. I was just Georgia, always there when you came home, always there to deal with problems while you were away.

'Part of that was my fault,' she went on, mindlessly shifting the spoons around the top bowl of the pile. 'I could have told you how I was feeling earlier. I could have refused to deal with everything until you realised just how much I did on top of my own job, but that would have been unreasonable of me. You were always away and when you came back I felt guilty for wanting your attention when you had so many more important things on your mind.'

'I would have listened to you,' Mac protested.

'How could I tell you that I was feeling resentful about things like leaking washing machines and problems with the bank when I knew that you'd been out in the middle of so much misery? That you were still thinking about the children you'd seen dying, about wars and famine and desperation? My concerns seemed so petty next to those. I'd decide to wait until the images weren't vivid, and you'd readjusted to life back home, but then the phone would ring, and you'd be off with your camera again.'

Mac's expression was rigid as he listened to her. 'So I was supposed to find out how you felt by telepathy, was I?'

'Look, I'm not saying it was all your fault,' Georgia said with something of a snap. 'I've just said that I was partly to blame. I decided that I might as well just get on with things, so I fell back into my old role of good old Georgia, she'll sort it all out. And once I got that job at the *Chronicle*, things improved. Being a feature writer might not have been as exciting as a hot-shot investigative journalist, but it least it was something that I could do for myself and, when I was there, I could be me. Not the Georgia that everyone in Askerby saw, and not the Georgia that *you* saw, but the me I felt myself to be. You don't know that me, Mac.'

'I think I do,' he said, getting to his feet and coming over to take the bowls out of her suddenly nerveless hands. 'I don't think you've changed as much as you think you have.'

He turned to put the bowls on the table and then took her hands. Georgia could feel the warmth and strength of his clasp jolt up her arms, while his fingers holding hers so tightly were enough to set alight the delicious tingle of skin against skin.

'There aren't three different Georgias, there's just one. And it's the same Georgia that I've loved ever since I first met you. She's tired, a bit battered by life, maybe, but she's still there.'

He paused, searching her face with his eyes. The navy blue gaze seemed to look deep inside her while Georgia struggled against the instinctive response to his touch that was uncoiling with terrifying speed inside her.

'Isn't she?' he said softly.

No. That was what she ought to say. *No, you're wrong, she's not there any more. It's just me, cool, crisp Georgia. I don't need passion and excitement, the wildness and the glory. I don't want it any more. I want a quiet, safe life.*

But the words stuck in her throat.

All at once, the fight drained out of Georgia. She couldn't tear her gaze away from his. All she could do was stand there dumbly, unable to look away, unable to lie.

Mac's heart contracted at her expression. He could see how much she wanted to lie to him, to insist that she had changed beyond all recognition, but she couldn't do it. She had always been so honest, so true. So beautiful. How could he have let her go?

His eyes dropped to her mouth. It had been too long since he had kissed her. Without thinking, his arms encircled her, pulling her towards him.

She could have resisted, Georgia knew that perfectly well, but she was just so tired of struggling. Mac's hands were warm against her, and his chest looked broad and inviting. She let him cup her face between his palms and when he lowered his mouth to hers she didn't even try to pull away.

His kiss was very gentle at first, his lips warm and sure and immensely comforting. Georgia had been alone a long time now. She had managed perfectly well on her own, but it was lonely at times. She hadn't let herself remember what it was like to be held, how good it felt to lean against a hard body and feel strong arms close around her.

After four years, he was still so familiar. In spite of his casual and sometimes downright scruffy appearance, Mac always smelt wonderfully clean. Georgia breathed in the scent of him and felt suddenly dizzy with memories of dark, delicious nights and long, lazy mornings. Of his hands drifting enticingly over her skin and his weight on her, of the feel of him and the taste of him, of the bone-melting, heart-shaking, breathtaking, intoxicating pleasure of their loving.

With a tiny sigh of release, Georgia gave in and relaxed against him, ignoring the sensible voice in her mind which was screaming *No! No! This wasn't supposed to happen!* It was just a little kiss. What could it hurt? It wasn't as if she was giving in. She was just…taking a little comfort for a while.

She gave herself up to the sheer pleasure of being held by Mac again, of tasting his mouth and slipping her arms around his waist so that she could spread her hands over the hard muscles of his back. When you looked at him he seemed lean and lazy, but she could feel the strength of him beneath her fingers and she was conscious again of the treacherous urge to rest against him and feel safe and secure.

It felt good, so good... *Too* good. Georgia
wasn't sure when the gentleness and the comfort
flickered into something deeper and more dangerous, but all at once those gentle sensations
were surging out of control as the old chemistry
between them re-ignited with a whoosh and their
kisses became harder, hungrier, more demanding.

Murmuring her name, Mac gathered her closer
and, dizzy with wanting him, Georgia clung to
him. She ran her hands over him, wherever she
could touch him, as they kissed and kissed and
touched and kissed again. Kissing, touching,
gasping with pleasure, she backed over to the
sofa, pulling him down with her, or perhaps he
pushed her down—it didn't matter. All that mat-
tered was the hard weight of his body, his hands
on her, the flex of his muscles and the taste of his
mouth.

Georgia gave herself up to spiralling sensation,
arching her body as Mac pushed up her top, his
fingers searing the softness of her skin, his mouth
hot against hers.

'Tell me now you're not the same,' he breathed
against her throat. 'Tell me there isn't something
special between us. Tell me that it isn't still
there.'

'I...can't,' Georgia managed.

'Then why resist it?'

Yes, why? Why, when it felt this good? Why,
when her body was throbbing, aching for him?

'Because it isn't enough.'

Slowly, painfully, reason filtered back into Georgia's brain, and she struggled into a sitting position. Pulling down her top, she smoothed back the hair that had come undone with shaking hands and took an unsteady breath.

'It isn't enough,' she said again, stronger this time.

Beside her, Mac had straightened too and was raking a hand through his hair, his blue eyes dark with frustration. 'We've got something special between us,' he insisted. 'You've just admitted it yourself. How can that not be enough?'

'I'm not denying a physical attraction—there's not much point in that after the last few minutes,' she admitted shakily, 'but that's all we've got, Mac.'

'The hell it is!' Mac glared at her, his jaw set furiously. 'I love you! And, what's more, I think you love me too!'

Georgia flinched as if from a blow. Somehow she managed to steady her breath and meet his eyes. 'Then you're wrong,' she said. 'You don't love me. You might want me, you might want the pleasure that we get together and you're right, it *is* special, but I'm not sure that you even see me,' she said. 'You think I'm still the person I was when I married you.'

'That's rubbish!' He bit back the angry words and made himself calm down before he spoke again, very carefully. 'Of course you've changed since then,' he said, 'but that doesn't change how I feel about you.'

Taking hold of her hands, he held them tightly, refusing to let her tug them free as he wondered how to convince her. 'I do love you, Georgia,' he said desperately. 'I've always loved you, and I know I was an idiot to let you go, but you're still my wife, and I want to be with you. My life is never going to be complete without you. Why can't we forget this divorce nonsense and try again?'

'Because you're still thinking about what *you* want, not what *I* want,' said Georgia wearily.

'I don't believe you really want to marry that pompous bore!'

'What I *want*,' she said fiercely, 'is for someone to look at me properly, to see me as the person that I am, not as the person they would like me to be, and you've never been able to do that.'

Mac bit back the angry retort that rose to his lips. 'You're not the only one who's changed over the past four years, Georgia,' he said tautly, but she wasn't to be convinced.

'You haven't changed, Mac,' she said. 'Look at you! You're still riding around on a motorbike, springing surprises, winding up serious people like Geoffrey... You've never grown up, Mac, and I don't suppose you ever will.'

'Being grown up is about more than driving around in a family saloon,' said Mac, stung.

'Yes, it's about taking responsibility for your own actions, and how they affect other people,' Georgia retorted. 'You've never done that. You've just done what you want to do and never mind the mess and muddle you leave behind because someone else will sort it out! Well, I'm not going back to that,' she said flatly. 'I've done enough sorting out other people's messes. I've looked after my parents, I've looked after Becca, I've looked after you, and now I'm looking after Toby. I want someone who can think about me, about what *I* want and *I* need for a change.'

Mac set his jaw. 'I'll do that.'

Georgia just shook her head slowly. If only he knew how much she wanted to believe him! But there had been too many times when he had disappointed her, too many times when she had told herself that love was enough and had given him another chance to be what she needed, only to feel disenchanted when he just went on being himself.

'I will,' he insisted.

'I'm sorry,' she said. 'I just don't believe that you can.'

'Is that a challenge?'

She sighed. 'This isn't a game, Mac.'

'Because it sounded like a challenge to me,' he said, ignoring her.

'All right,' said Georgia, losing patience suddenly. 'OK, take it as a challenge, if that's what you want. You've talked about loving me, well, now *prove* it! Show me that you've grown up and are capable of a serious relationship, that you're prepared to think about me and not just about yourself, and then I might—just *might*—reconsider our divorce.'

Mac wasn't about to let a chance like that go. It was the best offer he was going to get from Georgia for now, and he knew it.

Getting up, he went over to the leather jacket that he had slung over an armchair in spite of the fact that there were perfectly good coat hooks in the hall, and pulled a long legal envelope out of the inside pocket. 'Here are the divorce papers,' he said, dropping them on to the coffee table. 'Let's have a bet, shall we?'

A bet. The very word brought back a rush of memories.

I bet I can make you laugh first.

I bet you can't resist that ice cream.

I bet I love you the most.

Their marriage had had an undercurrent of competition that had kept their relationship sparking, because no matter how frivolous, tender or erotic the challenge, the truth was that neither of them had ever liked to lose.

'So what's the bet this time?' Georgia asked as coolly as she could.

'I bet that I can convince you that I love you

and can be what you need,' said Mac. 'And, what's more, I bet I can make you realise that you still love me.'

Georgia laughed. She couldn't help it. 'You'll never be able to do that!'

'That's the bet,' he said simply.

'Well, I bet you can't!'

'Fair enough. So now we have to agree what the winner gets—and I think we should keep it simple. If I win, you tear up those papers and we stay married. If you win...' Mac shrugged. 'I'll sign and the divorce will go straight through.'

Georgia rolled her eyes. 'Oh, this is ridiculous! We can't possibly make a bet like that!'

'Chicken?' said Mac provocatively.

She glared at him, knowing exactly what he was doing. She ought to refuse to have anything to do with something so silly. How could they possibly bet on their marriage, of all things? It was crazy.

And yet...old habits died hard. It went against the grain to turn down a challenge from Mac, especially with his blue eyes on her, waiting for her to give in.

And he couldn't win, she was sure of that. In an odd way, Georgia felt stronger after that kiss, devastating as it had been. It was a bit like surviving an accident. She had come dangerously close to succumbing completely, but now that she had pulled herself out of the spiral of lust, she knew that she could do it again and think sensibly once more. Not immediately perhaps, but she wasn't doing too badly, all things considered.

'Is there a time limit on this bet?' she said. 'I don't want to be hanging on indefinitely.'

'Why don't we say three months?' suggested Mac. 'If I haven't convinced you by then, then I think I'll have to accept that I won't be able to.'

Three months. She could easily hold out that long.

'All right.' Georgia met his gaze squarely, her own bright with challenge. 'You're on.'

CHAPTER FIVE

GEORGIA scrolled through the agency reports online, skimming through the latest stories from around the world. Political unrest, disasters, murders, scandals, coups. Big decisions were being made, the world was changing by the minute.

Except in Askerby. Askerby just went on having its vegetable shows and its car boot sales and limited its glaring headlines to rows about street lights or uproar over changes in the bus timetable.

Georgia sighed and closed the agency report window. It wasn't that she wanted bad news to come to Askerby. Of course she didn't want that. It was just that sometimes she wished that there was *some* news to report. It didn't have to be much. Just something interesting or exciting every now and then. Was that so much to ask?

Oh, well, she had told Mac that she wanted to settle for a quiet life now, so there was no point in complaining about it. If a quiet life was what you wanted—and she *did*—then Askerby was the place to be.

She was just feeling out of sorts because she

was tired, Georgia told herself. She hadn't slept well the night before, having spent the night tossing and turning and reliving the kiss whose memory still simmered and sizzled along her veins and left her feeling twitchy and itchy and hot.

It had been stupid to let Mac kiss her, and even stupider to kiss him back. So much for her Gloria Gaynor impression. She was supposed to be stronger than that now, and it wasn't as if she hadn't known at the time that it was madness.

But, oh, it had felt good...

And that bet! Georgia jerked her mind away from how wonderful that kiss had been. At least she had managed to stop it in time, but what was the point of being sensible then if she was going to accept a crazy bet like that? What on *earth* had she been thinking of?

Mac didn't like to lose any more than she did, and that meant that he would now be around for the next three months, reminding her of all the good times that they had had together, as if it wasn't hard enough for her already.

Why hadn't she just said no? Georgia wondered despairingly. She could have told Mac that there was no question of him being able to convince her that he loved her in the way she wanted to be loved. She could have told him to sign the papers and leave, and her life could have gone back to the way it was before.

But no! She had to go and accept his silly challenge. Surely—*surely*—there wasn't a bit of her that wanted Mac to win, was there? Surely there wasn't a bit of her that was that blind and foolish and willing to forget all the times in the past that he had let her down?

Georgia devoutly hoped not. In the cold light of morning she could remember the fact that a relationship based on nothing more than physical attraction couldn't last, as she had already learnt the hard way. There was no way she would be making that mistake again.

And Mac could try all he might, but he would never be able to convince her that he had understood what she needed. Georgia was sure of that. He might try to seduce her, to use the sexual chemistry between them, but she had meant it when she'd said that that was not enough for her.

No, this was one bet Mac wouldn't be able to win.

Georgia just wished she could feel more pleased about that.

Her eye fell on the time displayed at the bottom of her computer screen and she gave a muttered exclamation. It was almost ten. She should have been planning what she was going to say at the editorial conference this morning, not thinking about Mac.

Too late now, though. She would just have to play things by ear. Who knew, maybe somebody else would come up with some ideas for once?

Gathering up her notebook, pen and glasses, Georgia headed for the newsroom.

'Ready?' she said to Rose as she closed her office door, and then stopped when she saw who was lounging on the edge of Rose's desk.

Mac.

Oh, for heaven's sake, now her heart was going into that wild, somersault routine again, jumping into her throat and stopping her breath just when she most needed it. When would it learn not to *do* that?

'It's great news, isn't it?' Rose beamed. 'I'm sure Mac will be fantastic!'

Georgia found her voice with difficulty. It didn't sound much like her own voice, but it would have to do. 'Rose, would you mind going on ahead?' she managed. 'Tell the others I'll be there in just a moment.'

'Of course.' Rose jumped up eagerly. 'Shall I get you some coffee?'

'That would be kind, thank you, Rose.' Georgia waited until Rose had bustled out of earshot before rounding furiously on Mac. 'What are you doing here?' she demanded.

Mac raised his brows at her tone. 'You told me to come.'

'*What?* I did no such thing!'

'You promised to give me a trial as a photographer,' he reminded her. 'A month, you said.'

She *had* said something like that, but she hadn't expected him to take her seriously. 'I was joking!'

'Oh. Right.' Assuming an unconvincing chastened look, Mac straightened from his easy position against the desk. 'My fault for taking you seriously. So you don't really want a photographer after all?'

'Yes! No... Wait!' said Georgia as he hoisted his camera bag on to his shoulder and turned to go. 'Is this to do with our bet?' she asked him suspiciously.

Mac's eyes gleamed. 'You told me to think about what you needed,' he pointed out. 'And it seemed to me that what you need most at the moment is a photographer.'

'I was talking about emotional needs! You don't honestly think that snapping a few pictures for me will be enough to change my mind about a divorce, do you? I can tell you now that I'm not *that* desperate!'

Although she was pretty close, if the truth be known.

'Oh, filling in as a photographer is just the first shot in my campaign,' Mac admitted cheerfully. 'It seemed to me that if I was going to be here for three months, I might as well make myself useful, but if you don't want me around, I'll go.'

Georgia clutched her notebook to her chest and eyed him with resentment. He knew how much she needed a photographer, and to have someone of his calibre on the *Gazette*… What a coup it would be! His pictures would transform the look of the paper. She was aware of a flicker of excitement as she considered what having Mac around might mean.

He wouldn't stay, of course, but it would take him three months to realise that he wasn't going to win the bet, and that would give her time to find someone else. In the meantime he could train Gary, who would probably learn more in those three months than a year with anyone else.

It was a terrific solution to her problem, so how come she felt as if she had been out-manoeuvred? Mac had found the perfect way to stick around. He would always be there, always reminding her of what she had had, of what she could still have… But she could handle that, couldn't she?

Georgia squared her shoulders. She wasn't going to let him think that she was running scared.

'Very well, if you're happy to be temporary photographer, that would suit me,' she said. It was a struggle to sound cool but she didn't think she managed too badly.

Typically, Mac was totally unintimidated. He just grinned at her. 'Great.'

'But only on the understanding that you treat it as a proper job,' she warned, wishing his smile didn't make her nerves jump. 'You turn up like everyone else and take the pictures I tell you to.'

And stop smiling, she wanted to add.

'You're the boss,' Mac agreed.

'I am, so please don't forget it,' said Georgia coldly. 'Our relationship inside this building has to be strictly professional.'

'Naturally,' said Mac, who had indeed stopped smiling, not that it made much difference when his blue eyes were still glinting with humour.

Georgia sighed inwardly. She had tried to cover herself, but if she couldn't even cope with Mac straight-faced, she had a nasty feeling that it was all going to be a lot harder than anticipated.

Still, she had to look on the bright side. At least she had a photographer now.

'In that case, you'd better come along to the editorial conference,' she said.

The conference was held in a poky meeting room where the chairs were squeezed around a table scarred with generations of coffee cup rings. The one window looked out across the narrow yard to the blank end wall of the bank next door. It was not an inspiring view.

The others were all there, lounging around the table in various states of disarray. Kevin and Niles looked distinctly hung-over, and Cassie had the haphazardly dressed air of someone who had slept through the alarm and had only fallen out of bed five minutes ago.

Georgia eyed her team with disapproval. They were all so *slovenly*. She knew they thought she was the odd one out, with her elegant clothes and her manicured nails. She was always well-groomed, but to Georgia it was part of being professional. The casual standard of dress amongst the others depressed her, because it implied that they didn't take their jobs seriously.

Rose wasn't too bad, as she still had a huge wardrobe of expensive clothes from before her divorce, and Meredith, the accountant, always looked neat and precise, but the others…Georgia shook her head mentally. She would never be able to turn this paper around until this lot sharpened up their act.

They'd all stopped talking when she came in and were eyeing her warily, obviously waiting for her to spring yet another ambitious idea on them that would require a bit of effort on their part.

Georgia's heart sank. She was going to have to do something to create a team spirit, but what? Every attempt at including them in the decision-making was met with wary suspicion and a deep-rooted aversion to change. She had thought they would have leapt at the chance to transform the paper under the aegis of a young and innovative editor.

Wrong. The experienced staff had all walked out and she was left with those that were either too lazy to move or too inexperienced to know that things could be different.

Oh, well. If at first you didn't succeed….

'Good morning!' she said as brightly as she could.

'Morning,' they mumbled back, for all the world like a class of reluctant schoolchildren responding to their teacher.

They all had plastic coffee cups from the machine in front of them. The coffee was absolutely disgusting and Georgia often wished she had the nerve to bring in her own cafetière, but she was afraid that would just alienate them even more. So she just smiled her thanks when Rose set a cup down by her elbow.

Taking a sip, she tried not to grimace. It was boiling hot, bitter and tasteless all at the same time. Quite a feat.

The rest of the staff were staring with naked curiosity at Mac. God only knew what they would make of having a world class photographer in their midst. Perhaps that would seem like another threat?

To Georgia's annoyance, Mac didn't seem the slightest bit concerned to find himself the focus of all eyes. He smiled his lazy smile around the table and let Rose fuss around him, bringing him coffee too and making sure Kevin passed the biscuits.

'OK, everyone, let's start,' she said briskly to cover her nervousness, and put on her glasses. 'First of all, I want to introduce you to our new photographer, Mac Henderson. Mac's only here temporarily, but I think you'll be able to learn a lot from him, Gary,' she said to the gangling youth who sat shyly at the end of the table, head bent so that his hair flopped over his eyes and hid most of his face. 'Gary will be your assistant,' she told Mac when Gary only murmured something inarticulate.

'Great.' Mac smiled at him in a friendly fashion, while Gary gulped in alarm at being the centre of attention.

'Hang on.' Cassie sat up in her chair suddenly. 'Did you say Mac Henderson? As in *Mackenzie* Henderson?'

'That's me.'

'*The* Mackenzie Henderson?' Cassie stared at him. 'As in award-winning war photographer? I queued to see your exhibition when it came to Leeds last year. It was fantastic!'

'Thanks,' said Mac easily.

'If it's not a rude question, what are you doing in Askerby?' Cassie went on, and Georgia looked at her with new approval. Reporters were supposed to ask rude questions and it was the first time she'd seen Cassie show any of the curiosity natural to any journalist.

Mac smiled and glanced at Georgia, who sent him a warning look in return. 'Georgia and I are…old friends,' he began.

'Mac's kindly offered to help us out until I can find a permanent photographer to replace Chris,'

Georgia put in quickly before he could say anything else. She didn't trust him not to stir things up, and she wanted to make it clear that his role was a purely temporary one. 'He's obviously experienced, as you've pointed out, Cassie, but as far as the *Gazette* is concerned, he's just an ordinary member of staff.'

'That's right,' Mac confirmed with a grin that made it clear that whatever he might be, it certainly wasn't ordinary.

'I'll introduce you to the rest of the team,' Georgia went on coldly. 'Rose, you know already. She's my secretary and office manager, so if you've got a practical problem, go to her and she'll sort it out.'

By coming straight to Georgia with the problem, normally. Rose could be a bit ditzy at times and her arrogant, obnoxious husband had trampled her self-esteem into the dust before leaving her for a woman young enough to be their daughter, so she was inclined to double-check everything with Georgia, who ended up sorting things out herself because it was quicker that way.

The way she always did.

Maybe, thought Georgia, she should try just letting everyone make a mess of it on their own for a change?

'Next to Rose is Kevin,' she went on, and Kevin raised a casual hand in greeting. He was too indolent to have walked out in protest at

Georgia's appointment. 'Kevin's our sports reporter.'

'I do the motoring section as well,' said Kevin, as if it were a huge burden instead of an occasional column about cars.

Mac looked suitably impressed.

'Then we've got Meredith, who does all our accounts,' said Georgia, gesturing towards a prim-looking girl in glasses.

'Ah, you're the person to grovel to when it comes to paying my expenses,' said Mac with a smile that even Meredith couldn't resist. She smiled back.

'Not until you've grovelled to me to sign them first,' said Georgia, who knew she ought to be pleased that Mac was clearly going to have so little trouble settling in, but feeling put out instead that his effortless charm made it look so easy.

Cassie was next. 'Cassie is our only reporter at the moment,' Georgia explained to Mac, 'so the two of you will probably be working together a lot.'

'Sounds good to me,' said Mac, who liked Cassie's quirky, humorous face and bright eyes.

'I'm not just a reporter,' said Cassie with a mock-pretentious air. 'I also do features and travel and restaurant reviews,' she went on cheerfully. 'Oh, and the women's page. I used to do the horoscopes too but Georgia stopped them.'

'Spoilsport,' Mac said to Georgia.

'I let them keep Spot the Dog,' she said defensively.

'Spot the Dog?'

'It's a competition, like Spot the Ball, only in this version we give them a picture of some sheep in a field and delete the sheepdog from the photo,' Cassie told him. 'The readers have to mark where they think the dog is, and whoever's closest to the original wins the prize. It's huge round here. We run it every week and it gets more response than anything else.'

Mac began to laugh. He couldn't help it. Spot the Dog! Poor Georgia! It was a long way from the cut and thrust of Fleet Street. No wonder she was finding it hard going here. Her heart was in London, where the news just kept on coming, not on some Yorkshire hillside with a flock of sheep and an invisible collie.

'Will photographing the sheep be my responsibility?' he asked Georgia, still laughing.

'Gary does the pictures for Spot the Dog,' she said with a frosty look, well aware of why he was so amused. 'I'm sure he'd be happy to show you how he does it if you're interested!'

'I can't wait,' said Mac.

'Finally, next to Gary, we've got Niles,' Georgia ploughed on. 'Niles looks after all the advertising.'

And all the sexual innuendo, she felt like adding. Niles was in his late forties, with a slight paunch, and generally very pleased with himself. He had an oily manner about him that Georgia loathed, and he was constantly making comments that just verged on the right side of downright offensive, but she had to be careful not to offend him. As with all papers, the advertising was a vital part of their revenue, and slimy though he might be, Niles knew what he was doing at work. With things as precarious as they were at the moment, Georgia had no choice for now but to grit her teeth and put up with him.

'That's it?' said Mac, looking round the table. Seven people, eight including him, he supposed.

He thought of the Sunday paper Georgia had worked for in London in its glass and chrome building. There were rows of subs, a vast news-desk with constantly ringing phones, reporters ranged around the huge open plan room, and that was just in the news section. There was another whole area for features, the picture desk, for copy editors, a separate floor for sales and advertising, and another for management and administration. All those people to produce a paper that came out once a week just like the *Gazette* did, but Georgia had to manage with seven. It couldn't be easy for her.

Georgia squared her shoulders, reading his thoughts without difficulty. 'It's a small team,' she agreed, 'but we manage to get the paper out every Thursday.'

More used to comparing the Gazette unfavourably with the big nationals, she was for the first time conscious of a flicker of pride as she spoke. It *was* something to be proud of, she realised, and when she looked around the table she saw some nods of agreement.

She had tried to be careful, but perhaps her disparaging attitude to the *Gazette* had shown through, Georgia thought, suddenly ashamed. She had been going about this all wrong. Instead of trying to make the *Gazette* like a national paper, she should start with the advantages she had and build on them.

'Right, well, now we've done all the introductions, let's get on with the conference. Cassie, what are you doing today?'

Cassie consulted her notebook. 'Apparently there's been a spate of burglaries in Ulverton Road—I'll see what I can get out of my contact in the police about that. There's a rumour going round that the Council are going to sack its rat catchers, or vermin control officers as I gather we're supposed to call them now. Do you think that's worth following up?'

Georgia's burst of pride in the *Gazette* was fading fast. This was the hectic pace of news in Askerby. 'The rat catchers could make a story,' she said. 'Pollution, vermin out of control, health risks... Yes, see what you can find out. We can always make it an exclusive. Anything else?' she asked hopefully.

Preferably something interesting.

'The lollipop lady at St Chad's Junior School is retiring today. I thought I'd do a human interest story about her.'

Retirement of a lollipop lady. Dear God.

Georgia resisted the urge to bang her forehead against the table.

Cassie must have read her expression. 'The school will be really disappointed if I don't go,' she said. 'They rang me about her specially. Her name's Mavis Blunt. According to the head-teacher, she's been making sure that children can cross the road safely for thirty years. She's out there with her lollipop in all weathers, and they want to give her a good send off.'

'It's the kind of story people like,' Meredith agreed. 'And if you get lots of children in the photo with her, they'll all buy the *Gazette* to see themselves in the paper.'

Georgia sighed. They were right, of course. 'Yes, yes, do the lollipop lady,' she said. 'You'd better go with Cassie, Mac,' she added, rather enjoying the thought of the great Mac Henderson, more used to snapping presidents and prime ministers, using his talents on a school photo. 'It can be your first assignment for the *Gazette*!'

She felt less pleased with the idea when she saw Mac and Cassie head off together after the conference. She could see them laughing together through the glass between her room and the rest of the office.

It wouldn't last, Georgia told herself. The novelty of it all might have a certain appeal but Mac wouldn't be happy taking pictures like that day after day. After the lollipop lady assignment he was going with Gary to photograph a resident of Ulverton Road looking aggrieved outside his burgled home, and then on to a rugby match between two local colleges.

He would soon get bored and give up.

She had to admit that he didn't look bored at the moment, though. She watched as he shrugged on his leather jacket, listening to Cassie, who was talking animatedly while she wrapped a bright pink scarf round and round her neck. Cassie wasn't strictly pretty, but her vivid face and personality were very attractive.

Georgia bit her lip. She hoped they weren't going to get on *too* well. Of course Cassie wasn't thirty yet. She wouldn't have any interest in Mac, who must seem middle-aged in comparison.

Then Mac smiled down at Cassie and Georgia's heart clenched. His teeth were white, his smile crooked and the corners of his navy-blue eyes crinkled engagingly. He was tall and lean and hard. Cassie would have to be blind not to notice how attractive he was.

Not that she cared, Georgia reminded herself

sternly. She had already told Mac that she wasn't interested in restarting their marriage and he wasn't going to be able to change her mind, bet or no bet. He was just wasting his time if he thought he could.

Determinedly, Georgia turned her back on the friendly scene in the newsroom and scowled at the computer. She was supposed to be writing the editorial.

No suggestions about issues likely to grip Askerby had been forthcoming at the editorial conference and the blank screen gazed unhelpfully back at her. Perhaps she could whip the potential axing of the rat catchers into a crusade about rubbish collection?

Georgia rested her fingers on the keyboard and flexed them, ready for action, but the words wouldn't come. What she needed was inspiration.

She found herself remembering what Cassie had said about Mavis Blunt and how the school wanted to mark her retirement as something special. There must be lots of people who did little jobs in the community that were hardly noticed but which made a real difference to people's lives, she thought, and this time her fingers started moving over the keyboard of their own accord...

She didn't see Mac again until she was leaving that evening. It was raining and he was standing on the front step, pulling up the collar of his jacket before he set out into the wet. Her heart gave its usual lurch at the sight of him, but she managed to keep her voice composed as she came up behind him.

'What, no bike?' she said, noting the lack of helmet, and when he swung round at the sound of her voice his smile seemed to light up the dark, dreary evening.

'No, I left it at the hotel,' he told her. 'Cassie's been driving me around today.'

Somehow Georgia didn't really like the thought of him spending all day in the car with Cassie. 'Where are you staying?'

'The Grand.'

She raised her brows. The Grand was the most expensive hotel in town, although that was not saying much, it was true. 'I'm not sure your salary at the *Gazette* is going to run to the Grand for three months.'

'Oh, don't worry, I'm moving. Rose has got a friend who takes in paying guests, apparently, so I'm going to see her tonight. With any luck I can move in there tomorrow.'

Mac would belong in Askerby long before she did, Georgia thought with a trace of bitterness. Look at him, already on chatty terms with Rose and Cassie. It wasn't even as if he ever made a particular effort to be liked. People just did things for him anyway.

Just the way she had used to.

Well, not any more. If Mac was serious about wanting her back—and it was always hard to know with him whether he was being serious or not—then he would have to learn to make an effort for her. Until he worked that one out, he would never win that bet.

He might not be able to give her what she needed, but there was no need to be unfriendly. Georgia unfastened her umbrella and shook it out. 'The Grand's on the other side of town,' she said. 'I'll give you a lift, if you like. It's a horrible evening, and the car's just round the corner.'

'Are you sure that's allowed?' asked Mac with mock concern. 'We're still technically in the building, you know, and I wouldn't want to break our rule about keeping things strictly professional on the first day!'

'I *am* being professional,' said Georgia. 'I'd offer a lift to any member of staff in this weather.'

'Ah, well, that's put me in my place,' said Mac. 'But yes, please, I'd still like a lift. Why don't I take that umbrella? I'm a bit taller than you.'

A sensible idea, but Georgia hadn't counted on how intimate it would feel walking with him under the shelter of the umbrella. It was a very small space out of the rain and they had to walk close together, which wouldn't have bothered her in the slightest if it had been Geoffrey or Kevin or Gary. She might not have been so keen being so close to Niles, but even that wouldn't have disturbed her in quite the way that matching her pace to Mac's easy stride did.

'Those were wonderful pictures you took of the lollipop lady,' she said after a moment, uncomfortable with the silence but determined to keep the conversation neutral.

'Oh, you got them? Good.'

'I'm going to put the one of her bending down to talk to the little boy on the front page,' she told him. 'It's a fantastic photo. I don't know how it is one person can point a camera and just get a snap,' she went on thoughtfully, 'and when you do it, the picture tells a whole story.'

Mac stopped and, because he had the umbrella, she had to stop too, the two of them isolated under its shelter. He looked down at Georgia, her face tilted up to his, the beautiful grey eyes wary, while the rain pounded on to the umbrella, cascading off its edges and splashing on to the pavement around them, and for a long moment it seemed as if the rest of the world, the traffic and the passers-by hurrying under their own umbrellas, had receded into the distance, leaving the two of them quite alone.

'Thank you,' he said quietly. 'That's one of the nicest things you've ever said to me.'

'Oh, I'm sure I must have said nicer things than that,' said Georgia, trying to lighten the suddenly intense atmosphere.

'You used to say you loved me,' he agreed.

'Well, there you go.'

Jerking her eyes away, she began walking so that he would have to keep up with the umbrella. Anything was better than letting herself be trapped in his gaze like that. It only led to trouble.

Mac didn't speak again until they reached her car. 'Are you sure I won't be taking you out of your way?'

'No.' Georgia pointed her key to unlock the car, watching the lights flash and the door locks click up obediently. 'I've got to go to the supermarket to find something for supper, and that takes me right past the Grand.'

'What's on the menu for tonight?' Mac asked as they got in.

'I don't know,' said Georgia morosely. 'I always mean to draw up a shopping list, but then I can't be bothered and when I get there I just can't think of anything I can make at all!'

She slotted the key into the ignition. 'It's at times like this that I really miss that little Indian takeaway that we used to have round the corner in London. Do you remember it?'

'What, the one we had on speed dial on the phone?'

Georgia half laughed, half grimaced. 'I don't suppose it was very healthy. It was good, though. I wonder if they'd deliver up from London?' She sighed wistfully as she started the engine. 'I'd do anything for a curry like that again. There's fat chance of one in Askerby. It's not exactly a multicultural centre, as you've probably noticed.'

'Yes, it's very different from London,' said Mac, reaching for his seat belt.

'Everything's different,' said Georgia sadly.

'Not everything,' he said, as she put the car into reverse. 'Some things never change.'

She had turned to look behind her before backing out of her parking slot but, as she did, her eyes snagged on Mac's and all at once the world juddered to a halt. She sat frozen, her head twisted to one side, trapped by the dark blue gaze that held her immobile while the air between them jangled with memories.

Mac kissing her, Mac holding her, Mac telling her that he would always love her. And her, arching beneath his touch, wrapping herself around him, loving him completely... The memories were so vivid, they hurt.

They hurt so much, it was hard to breathe.

CHAPTER SIX

SOMEHOW, Georgia found the strength to break the look. Swallowing hard, she jerked her head further round and stared shakily at the rain splattering the rear window, feeling horribly flustered.

Oh, God, now she had lost reverse! She fumbled with the gearstick as she tried to get the car into gear once more. Get in...get *in*...at last!

The car jerked backwards, narrowly missing a cyclist without lights who had materialised through the rain and swerved violently around them before speeding off with a rude gesture.

'I'd forgotten that you drive the way you cook,' said Mac, his voice threaded with amusement. 'It's odd, when you're so good at everything else you do.'

Georgia gritted her teeth. 'I'm a perfectly good driver,' she said, wishing that she didn't sound quite so defensive, and wishing even more that she could get into first gear.

Mac considered that, his head on one side. 'No, I don't think I can agree you with there,' he said. 'You're a terrible driver—that's third, by the way, not first—and an appalling cook, but that's what I love about you. Everyone's got to have a chink or two in their armour.'

Deciding that it was better to ignore that with lofty indifference, Georgia found first at last and shoved the car into gear, at which point it began to bunny-jump forwards. Straight towards a parked car, in fact.

Infuriatingly, Mac didn't even bat an eyelid as she slammed the brakes on just in time and the car promptly stalled.

Right, she had to calm down. Georgia stopped, took her hands off the wheel, drew several deep breaths and started again.

This time all went well, and they made it to the junction with only a slight confusion between the indicators and the windscreen wipers to make a smile tug at the corner of Mac's mouth.

'You're making me nervous,' she complained, and then wished that she hadn't. Now he would ask her what possible reason she had to be nervous just because their eyes had met.

And he had kissed her last night.

And he had thrown her life into total and utter confusion.

No reason to be nervous because of that, was there?

'Anyway, tell me about your day,' she hurried on before he could venture into dangerous territory. 'How did you get on with the lollipop lady?'

Mac's face lit with enthusiasm. 'She was great! It's a long time since I've taken pictures of such a happy story. Mavis was wonderful, very quiet, very direct, but she had this big smile that made you feel that everything was all right.'

'Yes, I saw it in the pictures,' said Georgia, hugely relieved to have moved the conversation on to such safe territory. 'It was easy to see why the children all loved her.'

'They really did,' said Mac. 'They had made a huge effort to make sure that the party was a surprise, and they'd bought her a present and made her a cake. Mavis was almost in tears.' He smiled at the memory. 'It wasn't big news, it wasn't dramatic. It was just people being kind and appreciating each other.'

He paused. 'I know you didn't think it was much of a story, but it was, in its own quiet way. Maybe those are the stories people want to read in the *Gazette*.'

'Are you trying to tell me that I should stick to retiring lollipop ladies and Spot the Dog?' asked Georgia defensively.

'I don't mean you shouldn't keep people informed about what's going on locally,' said Mac carefully, 'but maybe you shouldn't feel so frustrated at the lack of exciting news. People can get that from the national papers. They want something different from the local rag.'

'Who says I'm frustrated?' snapped Georgia,

turning a little too sharply at the traffic lights. Oops, she had forgotten to indicate, too.

Mac just looked at her. 'I've known you a long time, Georgia, and I was watching you when you discussed possible stories in the conference this morning. You've got a much more expressive face than you realise.'

Georgia bit her lip. 'I wanted to make the *Gazette* different,' she confessed after a moment. 'I want it to be innovative, *exciting*. How can I do all that while we're still churning out the same old stories about scout groups or the uproar over new parking charges?

'Maybe it's not the content that matters as much as the quality of the writing and the design.'

'I suppose so,' said Georgia, sounding depressed. 'It's hard to do all that on your own, though.'

'You're not on your own. You've got a team. Not a very big one, admittedly, and not a very experienced one, but who knows what they could do if they were inspired?'

'They're not going to be inspired by me,' she said with a touch of petulance. 'It's obvious that they all resent me for taking over and losing Peter his job. They all hate me!'

Mac rolled his eyes. 'They don't hate you, Georgia. Rose certainly doesn't. She told me how you were the only person who would give her a chance when she suddenly found herself back on the job market, and how patient you've been with her while she's learning.'

'OK, maybe *Rose* doesn't hate me,' Georgia conceded grudgingly.

'Nor does Cassie. She said there have been lots of times when she's been late or muddled and missed deadlines when you'd have been perfectly justified in kicking her out, but you covered for her instead. And then there's Meredith, who knows she doesn't have the experience on paper to run the accounts, but you trust her anyway... None of them hate you. They admire you and respect you...and they're intimidated by you.'

'Intimidated?' Astounded, Georgia turned her head to stare at him until he calmly indicated some traffic lights coming up at speed and she hurriedly jerked her attention back to the road as she slammed on the brakes.

'Come on, Georgia,' he said, unperturbed by her erratic driving. 'You're very bright, you're beautiful, you're well-dressed, you've had a successful career in London and it's obvious that you're not over-impressed by Askerby. You make them feel provincial, and they don't like that.

'You probably seem like Superwoman to them,' Mac went on. 'They're not to know that you can't cook or that you're hopelessly anal about tidying up—or that your driving isn't that hot, either,' he added as the car jerked and jumped forward once more. 'I bet you try and do everything at the *Gazette* yourself, rather than let anyone else make a mess of it, don't you?'

Georgia stuck her chin in the air and didn't answer, but they both knew that he was right.

'If they knew what you were really like, they'd like you,' said Mac.

'I try to be friendly,' she said, hating the pathetic note in her voice. 'Why can't people *see* what I'm really like?'

She meant it as a rhetorical question and wasn't expecting an answer, but Mac gave her one anyway.

'You hide,' he said.

'What do you mean, I *hide*? I don't hide!'

'Yes, you do. You put up this brisk, capable front so that no one ever realises that behind all that competence you're just as scared and hopeless as everyone else.'

'Oh, free counselling now?' snapped Georgia, deeply annoyed by this stage. 'Excellent! Perhaps you'd like to write a problem page in your spare time? We could get everyone to write in and get advice from Uncle Mac, you being such an expert on relationships and all!'

As usual, Mac was infuriatingly unfazed by her sarcasm. 'You asked the question,' he pointed out.

Georgia stomped round the supermarket, feeling crosser and crosser every time she thought about Mac's glib analysis. He was a fine one to talk about hiding! At the first sign of difficulties in their marriage, he had run off with his camera rather than talk to her.

And now he had the nerve to turn up when she was facing up to reality at last—*not* hiding, in fact!—and obviously expected her to fall back into his arms without making the slightest effort to understand why their marriage had fallen apart in the first place. Well, if Mac thought that pointing out the flaws in her personality was the way to win his bet and win her back, he was going about it all wrong!

But as the days passed there was no sign that he was the slightest bit concerned about the bet. At first prepared to repulse such obvious strategies as flowers or invitations to dinner, Georgia was perversely put out when none were forthcoming. She didn't even have the satisfaction of saying 'no' and proving how determined she was to resist him.

As it was, no one would guess that Mac had any interest in her at all, she thought, vaguely aggrieved.

Although she was relieved, naturally.

It wasn't that she *wanted* him to woo her, to try and seduce her with his lips and his hands and his smile. She had told him that she wasn't going to succumb to the undeniable physical attraction between them again, and very glad she was that Mac appeared to have got that particular message.

Very glad.

It made everything much easier for her that he had apparently accepted her decision, so of course she was glad.

But still. He might have tried *something*. Why hang around if he was just going to ignore her?

Anyone would think that he was enjoying working at the *Gazette*. Through the glass wall of her office, Georgia would see him laughing and chatting with the others in the newsroom. The atmosphere on the paper had improved dramatically since he had arrived. It felt relaxed and friendly. Only Georgia, shut away in her editor's cubicle, felt out of it.

Everyone liked Mac. Rose adored him. 'He's so kind and funny,' she told Georgia, bringing her yet another cup of undrinkable coffee. She seemed to think that Georgia couldn't survive without it and, rather than hurt her feelings, Georgia had taken to pouring it into the pot plant in the corner when she wasn't looking.

Oddly, the pot plant seemed to be thriving.

In spite of herself, Georgia's eyes shifted to the newsroom, where Mac was sitting with Gary at the 'picture desk', both of them absorbed with whatever was on the computer screen in front of them. It might be a great photograph, or it might be a computer game. You could never tell with Mac.

Georgia made herself look away. 'You're a free

agent, Rose,' she reminded her. 'If you like him so much, why don't you tell him?'

'Oh, I'm much too old for Mac! I'm forty nine.'

'So? Mac's forty-five. It's not a huge difference, is it? And you're a very attractive woman.'

Georgia wasn't just saying it. Rose had obviously been lovely when she was younger and she was still pretty, with soft blonde hair, beautifully cut, and warm blue eyes. She could be a bit ditzy, but for someone whose whole life had fallen apart without warning when her wealthy husband had summarily replaced her with a trophy wife and refused to pay maintenance on the grounds that all their children had left home, she was coping pretty well.

'Well…thank you,' said Rose gratefully. 'But, to be honest, I don't think I'm ready for all that yet. After twenty-seven years with Justin, I still can't imagine being with anyone else.'

'I know, it's hard,' said Georgia, thinking about how long it had taken her to contemplate another relationship after Mac. And look how difficult she was finding it to make any progress on that!

'Anyway,' said Rose with a sly look, 'it's pretty obvious that it's not me that Mac is interested in!'

Georgia went cold all over. If he wasn't interested in Rose, and he certainly wasn't interested in *her*, that only left Meredith and Cassie.

Meredith might appeal to him because she wasn't that dissimilar to Georgia, apart from being a good fifteen years younger with beautiful skin, unmarked by a single line that Georgia could see.

And then there was Cassie, who was younger too, and was much more fun. Or he could have met someone out on an assignment. Why had she ever let him leave the office?

'Oh?' she managed, as carelessly as she could. She didn't want to ask but she had to know. 'Who do you think he's got his eye on?'

'Well, it's obvious, isn't it?'

No, no, it wasn't obvious *at all*! Georgia set her teeth and forced herself not to shout at poor Rose.

'Is it?'

'It's you he watches,' said Rose.

To Georgia's dismay, her first reaction was one of dizzy, giddy relief. *Not* a good sign in someone who was supposed to be moving on and leaving him behind. A very *bad* sign, in fact.

'Oh, I don't think—' she began feebly.

'Yes, he does,' said Rose, who could be surprisingly shrewd just when you least expected it. Or wanted it, come to that. 'He watches you whenever he thinks you're not watching him.'

Involuntarily, Georgia's eyes went back to Mac, just as he looked up from the computer screen and caught her glance through the glass

wall for a jarring moment before Georgia managed to jerk her gaze away.

'A bit like that,' said Rose. 'Will there be anything else?' she asked innocently as the colour
rose in Georgia's cheeks.

'No, thank you, Rose,' she said stiffly. That
was *quite* enough.

What a ridiculous idea! Georgia thought when
Rose had gone. Of course she didn't watch Mac!
OK, she might notice if he was in the newsroom
or not, but she could hardly avoid that with a
whacking great glass wall in her office, could she?

Georgia wished it wasn't there, and then she
could get on with her work without her secretary
commenting on what she did and who she
watched—although how Rose could tell from her
desk by the door, behind a solid wall, Georgia
didn't know.

What did Rose know, anyway? she thought
crossly. Her secretary was outright wrong about
Mac watching her, so obviously she was wrong
about everything else too!

Apart from that one brief glance, Mac gave no
indication that he was aware that Georgia was
there at all. Occasionally he would come and lean
in her office doorway while they had a completely
impersonal discussion about his assignments for
the next few days, and then he would disappear
with Gary, often accompanied by Cassie, or occasionally Kevin.

Which was fine by Georgia. As long as he kept those great pictures coming, he could do what he liked, she decided, and if he had been distracted and had forgotten that stupid bet, so much the better.

That was what she told herself, anyway. It left her free to get on with her own life.

Of course, that life was pretty dull at the moment, revolving as it did around working in her lonely little office and picking Toby up from the After School Club.

On the basis of no evidence whatsoever, Georgia imagined Mac enjoying convivial evenings in the pub, or going out for meals with people like Cassie and Kevin, who were unencumbered by responsibilities, while she struggled to shop and cook and clean and clear up after Toby and fret about the amount of time he spent at his computer instead of playing with other children. By the time she got him into bed at night, she was too tired even to read.

It wasn't even as if Toby appreciated the effort. He was as quiet and withdrawn as ever. Sometimes Georgia wished that he would shout and argue and be bolshy like other boys his age, although she had no idea how she would cope with that on top of everything else.

The responsibility of caring for him was exhausting, but there were rewards too. They were getting used to each other and, although Toby wasn't a tactile child, sometimes he submitted to a hug or let her ruffle his hair, and if she could coax a smile out of him she felt as if she had conquered Everest.

So it wasn't a very exciting life, but Georgia concentrated on Toby and told herself that it was enough. And one advantage of being so tired every night was not having the time to think about Mac.

Much.

It was absolutely typical of Mac that he waited until she had convinced herself that he had completely forgotten the bet before he knocked on her door. Georgia was sitting at her desk, editing Kevin's latest report on the fortunes of the local football team and wondering what was so difficult about learning how to use the apostrophe.

'Come in,' she called, and then had to put up with her heart doing its usual gymnastics as Mac appeared. Instead of lounging in the doorway the way he usually did, he came in and shut the door behind him, smiling in a way that set all her nerves aflutter.

'I thought you were out,' she said foolishly, and then cursed herself for sounding as if she was keeping track of his movements. Watching him, as Rose would say.

'I've been out,' said Mac. 'I've taken a photo of some firemen posing with a cat they rescued from a tree yesterday, and now I've come back.'

'Oh. Right. Good.' Now it appeared she could only talk in one word sentences. Excellent, just the impression of cool professionalism that she wanted to convey! Georgia cleared her throat and tried again. 'What can I do for you?' she asked, relieved to find that she was capable of stringing a whole six words together after all.

'You can come and have coffee with me.'

It was the last thing Georgia had been expecting after all this time when he had kept their conversations strictly businesslike. 'Coffee?' she repeated cautiously.

'Yes, you know, the stuff you drink out of a cup, whizzed up with frothy milk,' said Mac. 'You can take half an hour off, can't you? Look, it's a lovely day,' he said, gesturing at the window, 'and there's a place that does good coffee down by the river.'

'I don't know...I've got to finish editing Kevin's piece,' Georgia prevaricated, shocked by how much she wanted to go.

'Give it back to him and make him put in his own full stops,' Mac advised. 'He knows where they go. He's just sloppy because he knows that you'll correct it all for him. Come on,' he urged, leaning both hands on her desk and subjecting her, most unfairly, to the full impact of his smiling blue eyes. 'The *Gazette* isn't going to grind to a halt if you have half an hour off and, besides, I want to show you something.'

Georgia took off her glasses as an excuse to look away from him. 'What is it?'

'Oh, I can't give it to you here,' he said with mock virtue. 'It wouldn't be professional!'

Was this about the bet? Georgia fiddled with her glasses, her heart galloping. She was uncomfortably aware that her mood had lightened at the mere thought that Mac hadn't forgotten after all and, while she knew that she was being contrary and illogical, suddenly she longed to be away from this cramped, dreary office for a while.

'Well, why not?' she said, managing what she hoped was a cool smile that gave no hint of the turmoil inside her.

Cool was the last thing she felt as she picked up her bag and left the office with Mac, avoiding Rose's eye. She felt excited and at the same time ridiculously shy, as if she were going out on a first date rather than walking along next to her husband. Her *estranged* husband, she reminded herself.

Not that she should have needed reminding.

As Mac had pointed out, it was a beautiful spring day. The sunshine was warm in the absence of the brisk wind that usually blew down from the hills and whipped smartly around the town, and there was a softness to the air. You could practically see the blossom opening on the cherry trees, while the willows on the far side of the river were shimmering in fresh, delicate green as their leaves unfurled.

Mac was taking pictures as he went along—second nature to him, and in the past it had annoyed Georgia that he seemed more interested in what he saw through his viewfinder than in talking to her. On this occasion, though, she was glad not to have to make conversation. Her mouth was so dry she wasn't sure that she would have been capable of it anyway.

Making the most of the sunshine, the café had put tables and chairs out on a small terrace overlooking the river, and everyone was trying hard to pretend that it wasn't a novelty.

'Perhaps we should do a feature on new pavement café culture in Askerby,' said Georgia as they found a table. It was a relief to be able to think of something to say. 'We could show that you don't need to go all the way to the Mediterranean to get a bit of Continental living!'

'Ah, but you can't beat the Med, as I'm sure Geoffrey would tell you,' said Mac, hanging his jacket on the back of his chair. Beckoning over a pretty waitress, he ordered a cappuccino for Georgia and an espresso for himself.

'How do you know I wanted a cappuccino?' said Georgia, seizing at the irritation.

'You always used to drink cappuccinos,' he said.

'My tastes might have changed, for all you know!'

'Have they? Would you like me to order you a black coffee? Something else?' Mac made to call back the waitress, until Georgia stopped him. She didn't want to end up drinking her way through a black coffee.

'No, a cappuccino's fine,' she said, feeling ridiculous and resenting Mac for it. 'Just…don't make assumptions.'

'What, even if they're right ones?'

'Especially then,' said Georgia through her teeth, annoyed, but at the same time relieved to have got over that stupid shyness.

Mac leaned back in his chair and regarded her indulgently. 'So, talking of the Med, how *is* Geoffrey these days? I haven't seen him around much.'

Neither had Georgia, although she wasn't about to tell Mac that. 'He's fine,' she said. 'Very busy. He's got a big project on.'

She had no idea what the project was, but it seemed to consume all Geoffrey's attention recently. Even when Ruth did let him out of the office, he was usually too tired to want to deal with Toby and made what Georgia was sure were excuses to stay at home. Given her own insistence that they didn't make their relationship a serious one until her divorce was resolved, she was hardly in a position to object, but she couldn't help resenting him a little. How could he take her mind off Mac if he was never there?

On the couple of occasions when they had managed to meet up, Geoffrey had been preoccupied and Georgia irritable and bored, a fatal combination. It made her sarcastic, which didn't go down very well with Geoffrey, but really, he wasn't helping. Georgia knew that she was being selfish, but she needed him to be kind and attentive and remind her of why it had seemed such a good idea to get divorced and think about making a life with him instead, because right now, with the sun on her shoulders and Mac smiling at her over the table, it was hard to remember.

Hard to remember, too, why she had been irritated a moment ago.

'So…'

Her eyes were slithering all over the place, and she found that she couldn't meet Mac's gaze. She hated the way it could pin her down. It always felt as if he were looking right inside her and if he did that now, he would see…what?

Georgia didn't want to think too hard about the shiver of anticipation that was snaking through her at the thought that Mac might be making a move at last. In particular, she certainly didn't want to think about why it was anticipation she was feeling and not exasperation, or preferably indifference, which was certainly what she *ought* to be feeling right now.

'So, what have you got to show me?' she asked in a not very successful bid to sound brisk and unconcerned.

'Ah, yes.' Mac waited until the waitress had set their coffees on the table in front of them before he twisted round in his chair and retrieved a blank envelope from the inside pocket of his jacket. He laid it on the table between them with an air of suppressed excitement. 'This is for you,' he said.

Georgia looked at it without touching it, suddenly nervous now that the moment had come. She moistened her lips. 'That's very sweet of you, but honestly, I've got lots of envelopes at the office!' she tried to joke.

Mac laughed. 'Take a look inside,' he said, and pushed it towards her.

Very slowly, almost reluctantly, Georgia picked up the envelope. Very conscious of Mac's eyes on her, she turned it over and eased her thumb under the flap, opening it carefully.

Inside was a plane ticket.

She pulled it out and opened it. Ms G Maitland was booked on a flight to Lima in less than three weeks.

'We'll fly out together,' said Mac eagerly, his face alight. 'We can spend a couple of nights in Lima and then head up to the mountains. We'll walk the last part of the Inca Trail and you can see the sun rise over Macchu Pichu. It'll just be the two of us and the mountains. You'll love it.

You know, you always said that you wanted to see Macchu Pichu at dawn,' he reminded her. 'This will be your dream come true! We can—'

He broke off, belatedly registering the look on Georgia's face. She was putting the ticket back in the envelope, pushing it back over the table towards him.

'What's wrong?' he asked her in disbelief.

'I can't go to Peru, Mac.'

'But it's only a short trip,' he protested, still finding it hard to comprehend her reaction. 'And you need a break. You were saying how tired you were the other night. I'm sure the others could manage to get the paper out without you for one week. It might be a bit chaotic, but it would do them good, and they'd appreciate you more when you got back!' he said in an attempt to cajole a smile out of her.

'It's not just the *Gazette*. I've got Toby to think about, too.'

'Well, yes…but couldn't you find someone to look after him just for a week?'

'He's not a budgie, Mac. He's a small boy, and it's not just a question of making sure that he has food and water!'

Georgia's throat was tight. It was humiliating to realise how desperately she had wanted Mac to get it right, how bitter it was to discover how badly he had got it wrong—again.

'Toby's going through a difficult patch at the

moment,' she tried to explain. 'There's some problem at school, I think, but I can't get him to talk about it. I can't just swan off to Peru and leave him to it.'

'Well, then…we'll take him with us,' said Mac a bit wildly, unable to believe that the wonderful surprise he had planned for her could be going so disastrously wrong. He had been so sure that she would be delighted that he had remembered her long-held dream.

'We can't take him with us,' said Georgia, letting the anger seep into her voice. Anger was so much easier to deal with than disappointment. 'Toby has to go to school and, even if he didn't, how do you think a small boy of eight would cope with the Inca trail? It's all I can do to get him to walk to the car!'

There was a ghastly silence.

Mac's face was set and she bit her lip, wanting, in spite of everything, to make it easier for him. Wanting him to understand.

'Look, Mac, that ticket… It was incredibly generous, but you must see that I can't accept it,' she said, cupping her hands around her cappuccino to stop them trembling.

'No, actually, I *can't* see that.' The blue eyes were hurt and angry. 'You *said* I should think about what you wanted and needed. You said you'd love to see Macchu Pichu, you've always said that. And you need a break. You said that too,' he accused her.

'I know, but...' Georgia pushed her cup away and pressed her fingers to her temples. 'When I said that I wanted you to think about what I need,' she started again, more slowly, 'I wanted you to think about my life *now*. Yes, I used to be able to drop everything and go somewhere exciting, and I loved it. If you'd booked a holiday like that to surprise me five years ago, I would have been over the moon. I needed that then, but you didn't do it then, did you?'

Mac said nothing, but a muscle in his cheek was twitching with furious tension.

'And *now*, now I need something different. Of course I'd still like to see Macchu Pichu, but I can't just drop everything and go now. I bet you never even thought about *my* plans before you booked those tickets!'

Mac unclenched his teeth with difficulty. 'It wouldn't have been a surprise if I had asked for your diary!'

'No, but you would have seen that there's a PTA meeting at school the night we were supposed to be arriving in Lima. I need to be there for Toby. And two days later, I've got a meeting with Griff Carver. Without him, I wouldn't have a job at all, and he's not the kind of man you change your appointments with at the last minute.'

'So that's it then?'

'I...yes.'

Mac picked up the envelope, his mouth a grimly compressed line. 'In that case, I'd better cancel everything.'

To her horror, Georgia realised that tears of disappointment were shimmering in her eyes and she turned her head to stare fiercely at the river, blinking the humiliating evidence of how much she had secretly hoped for away.

'You know, I really wanted you to do something wonderful,' she said after a moment. 'Something that showed that you had thought, really *thought*, about me.'

'That's what I was trying to do,' said Mac bitterly.

'I know, but you weren't really thinking about me at all. You were thinking about what would be exciting and fun and that you would enjoy doing for me. If you were trying to convince me that you truly loved me, then I'm sorry, but you didn't succeed.'

Mac's face seemed set in stone. 'So it seems.'

'I'm sorry,' said Georgia again, feeling angry and miserable at the same time.

She hadn't wanted to pour cold water on his idea, but why couldn't he *think*? It was like their marriage all over again—Mac full of fun and grand plans while she was tied up with domestic details, the boring, everyday business of running a home and holding down a job at the same time. She should have known this would happen.

Anyway, it looked as if she had won the bet. Funny how that didn't seem much comfort as she lay in bed that night, dry-eyed and staring at the ceiling.

Mac would go away again now, just the way she had wished that he would when he had first reappeared, and she would be left with the life she had said that she wanted, a life that stretched ahead, bleak and flat and joyless, for yet more years.

She felt just as she had in the early days of their separation, four years ago. Right back to square one, in fact. The same cold hard stone of misery was settling back into its old place inside her, somewhere between her heart and her stomach.

It hadn't been fair of Mac to come and do this to her, Georgia thought wretchedly. She had been happy before—well, happy enough—and now she was going to have to get over him all over again.

Well, she had done it before and she would do it again.

It was probably all for the best, anyway, Georgia tried telling herself. If that silly bet had gone on, she would have got more and more involved. The end result would have been just the same, only she would have been even more hurt and even more disappointed.

No, much more sensible to call a halt to it now and both accept the inevitable: that they had loved each other and been happy together, but now it was well and truly over.

CHAPTER SEVEN

HAVING made her decision, Georgia should have felt better, but somehow it didn't work that way. She was constantly on tenterhooks, waiting for Mac to come and tell her that he was leaving, and every time he appeared in the newsroom she would steel herself to get through the conversation that never happened.

Because Mac just carried on exactly as before. He turned up in the newsroom the next day, and proceeded to discuss the day's assignments with her as if nothing whatsoever had happened. Georgia didn't have the nerve to ask him when he was thinking of leaving. She couldn't face another conversation like the one they had had over coffee by the river. She just wished that he would make up his mind and let her know one way or the other so that she could stop being grouchy and get on with her life.

In the end, she got fed up with waiting. She couldn't put her life on hold until Mac deigned to inform her what he planned to do, so she was just going to have to get on with it.

As before, Georgia found solace in work. Oddly enough, after her initially negative response to the lollipop lady story, it was feedback from the editorial she'd written about Mavis Blunt that helped her the most. As a result of what she had written, letters came pouring in with suggestions of other unsung heroes and heroines in the community.

Georgia was so touched by some of the stories that she instigated a regular feature and called it Meet the Stars. Mac took a series of wonderful portraits that she was sure could form the basis for an exhibition one day, and Cassie was enthusiastic about the interviews, gaining enough confidence to begin suggesting other ideas for features.

Very gradually, the editorial conference became more animated, with other suggestions for stories being put forward. Some were so off-beam that Georgia boggled privately and avoided Mac's eyes, but she was careful not to ridicule any contributions.

She was pleased that the staff were feeling more committed to the *Gazette*. She suspected that a lot of the change in atmosphere was to do with Mac, whose photographs had already attracted notice, but she was working quietly on the design too, so that the paper began to look subtly different. It would be too much to say that she was feeling excited by what was happening, but at least her plan to transform the *Gazette* into an innovative example of local journalism at its best didn't seem *quite* as unattainable as it had before.

Before Mac arrived, a little voice inside Georgia would point out, but she would always push the thought aside. It was hard enough trying to ignore Mac's constant, vivid presence without having to give him credit for the very changes which were helping her to cope with it.

The atmosphere in the newsroom might have improved, but it was still not exactly chummy, and conversations tended to be stilted—at least with her. Nobody seemed to have any problem chatting away to Mac, she couldn't help noticing.

Georgia missed the camaraderie of the newspapers she had worked on in London, and tried to think of a way to recreate some of the same feeling in Askerby, but it was hard. A weekly outing to the pub was the obvious idea, but that didn't work for her. She had to pick up Toby after work. He had to spend enough time in After School Club as it was, and she would feel guilty about abandoning him again for an evening every week.

Then a meeting with Griff Carver gave her an idea. She was ridiculously nervous about suggesting it at the next morning's conference.

'Um…as some of you may know, I met Mr Carver yesterday,' she began.

'He does like to keep tabs on us, doesn't he?' murmured Mac.

'It's his paper,' Georgia pointed out in a frosty voice. 'He's entitled to know what's going on and, as it happens, he's very pleased with the way things are going. He particularly liked that piece you wrote about the Council's entertainment budget, Cassie, and he's been following Kevin's football reports with a lot of interest.'

Griff had made some pretty caustic comments about Kevin's writing style at the same time, but Georgia thought that she would keep those to herself. Kevin needed encouragement at the moment. Griff had also congratulated her on landing Mac as a photographer, but Mac didn't need confidence building like the others. He had more than enough confidence as it was.

She cleared her throat and went on. 'I don't know how many of you are aware of it, but Griff Carver is a generous supporter of the local hospice. He pointed out that the annual fund-raising ball is coming up, so I suggested we did a piece about it in the *Gazette* to push ticket sales.'

'Good idea,' said Rose. 'It's the kind of article that people like to read, and you could make a nice spread with some photos after the ball. You could even sell them, perhaps.'

'Rose, that's brilliant!' Cassie applauded. 'I bet people would pay through the nose for a portrait by Mackenzie Henderson. It would be a great way of raising extra funds.'

'And excellent PR for the *Gazette*,' added Georgia. She made sure she had her coolest expression in place before she looked at Mac. 'How would you feel about that?'

'Fine by me,' said Mac. 'When is this ball?'

'The end of the month. In fact,' said Georgia, taking a deep breath, 'I wondered how you would all feel about taking a table at the ball? We could all go and make it a staff social event…only if you wanted to, of course…'

She trailed off miserably and picked up her coffee, braced for rejection. Why would they all want to spend an evening with her, after all? They were probably all avoiding each other's eyes and trying to think up polite excuses and—

'That would be great!'

'I could wear my red dress.'

'Should be a good meal anyway—as long as no one expects me to dance!'

Far from squirming with embarrassment, they were leaning forward animatedly, talking to each other across the table.

'Can we bring a partner?' Mac's question cut across the hubbub, and they turned as one to look at Georgia.

'I don't see why not,' she said, wondering if he was thinking about asking her in front of everyone else. What would she say? Georgia didn't know whether to feel pleased or annoyed at such a public demonstration of his interest in her. As far as the others knew, they were no more than old friends, although the more curious among them might have wondered why such supposed good friends spent so little time together.

'Did you have anyone in mind?' she asked, cool as you like.

'Yes,' said Mac. 'I thought I'd ask Frances. Is that OK?'

Georgia's easy smile slipped for a fraction of a second before she hastily stuck it back in place.

'Frances?' she said, the temperature of her voice plummeting to arctic levels in spite of herself.

'My landlady.' Mac sounded surprised that she didn't know. 'She's great,' he said enthusiastically. 'Really good fun and a fantastic cook. I don't think she gets out much since she's been widowed, and she might like to come to the ball. What do you think, Rose? You know her better than I do.'

'I'm sure she'd love it,' said Rose with an approving look.

'Oh.' Georgia couldn't imagine an elderly widow particularly enjoying a noisy dinner dance, no matter how much fun she was, but she supposed it was kind of Mac to ask her. 'Well…invite her by all means, if you think she'd like it.'

'I could ask Simon if he wants to go,' said Cassie excitedly.

'I won't have a partner,' said Rose a little wistfully. 'I can't think of anyone I could invite.'

'I'll dance with you, Rose,' said Mac. 'You can be my partner.'

Rose flushed with pleasure, but reminded him that he had already said that he was going to invite Frances.

'I'll take you too.' He winked. 'I don't mind turning up with two gorgeous women. Think what that'll do for my reputation!'

'What about you, Georgia?' Cassie asked, and all eyes promptly swivelled back to where Georgia sat at the head of the table, trying not to look peeved by the way Mac was laying on the charm for everyone but her.

There was no way she was going to have anyone thinking that she hoped Mac would offer to include her in his cosy threesome. Georgia lifted her chin in a characteristic gesture. 'I'll ask Geoffrey,' she said.

Mac's eyes gleamed. 'Good idea,' he said.

Good idea? What did he mean, *good idea*? Georgia fumed as she stalked back to her office when the conference was over. It was hardly any time since Mac was claiming to be in love with her. He should be gnashing his teeth with jealousy at the thought of Geoffrey being lucky enough to sit next to her at the dinner, Geoffrey who claimed the last dance, Geoffrey who got to take her home in the dark at the end of the evening. But no! Mac thought it was a good idea for her to include him.

And what was he doing, commenting on her choice of partner, anyway? Georgia slammed her door and dumped her notebook on to her desk with a resounding thump.

He had obviously already abandoned the idea of convincing her that he loved her. She had thought it would take more than one setback for him to give up on the bet, but apparently not.

Not that she cared, obviously.

And that was absolutely *not* the reason she felt so low all week. It had nothing to do with Mac. She was just tired and irritable and frazzled by a week in which just about everything that could go wrong, did go wrong.

Cassie wasn't well, which meant that Georgia had to write most of the stories as well as edit them. Machines broke down as soon as she looked at them. Her computer, her car and her washing machine all chose that week to play up, although sadly the vending machine in the newsroom remained impervious to the negative force field she seemed to be carrying around with her, and kept on spewing out the liquid laughingly labelled 'coffee'.

And it wasn't just technology that went wrong. Toby was fractious, the bank officious and if she asked anyone at work to do the simplest thing they either forgot or made a mess of it so that she ended up having to do it all herself.

Oh, and it rained all week. Not just a few April showers, but a grey, sullen, drenching rain that wept continually from the clouds that lowered oppressively over the rooftops of Askerby, blocking out the sun and generally giving a very impressive rehearsal for the end of the world.

Georgia had had enough by Wednesday night, when she finally managed to put that week's edition of the *Gazette* to bed.

That day had been par for the course for the whole week. Not only had the office computers crashed, but Rose had got waylaid by the local conspiracy theorist at the door on her way back from lunch and had spent two hours being harangued about an international plot to test a truth drug on the population of Askerby. Quite why Askerby had been selected for this dubious distinction was never quite established but, while Rose had been cornered, Georgia had had to answer all the phones and, as a consequence, hadn't been able to concentrate on anything else.

Mac, she'd noticed, had made sure she had all the pictures she wanted and had strolled off at half past three, leaving Gary in charge of the picture desk in case of any emergency.

That had only made Georgia feel worse. She'd snapped at Geoffrey when he'd rung in the middle of a yet another crisis, and then the car had had to be coaxed into starting, which meant that she'd been later than ever picking Toby up from the After School Club.

'You're *late*,' said Toby sullenly.

'I know, I'm sorry, Toby, but—'

'You're always late.' He scowled. 'I have to stay here in this stupid club every day, and I hate it and I hate *you*!'

Georgia knew that he was only saying it because he was upset, but she had to struggle against the childish urge to burst into tears. But one upset child was quite enough to deal with just then.

'Toby,' she said after a moment. 'What's the matter? Has something happened?'

But Toby just turned his face away and refused to answer.

Not seeing anything to be gained in sitting outside the school trying to force him to talk to her, Georgia sighed and drove home. Now she could top off her foul mood with a good dollop of guilt. Just what she needed.

The headache which had been tightening behind her eyes all day was pounding by the time she eventually parked outside the house. Toby disappeared up to his room without a word, and while Georgia knew she ought to go after him and find out what was wrong—or more wrong than usual—she simply didn't have the energy.

She was tired and hungry and miserable, and she wanted someone to hold her and tell her that it would all be all right. Or, failing that, a hot bath with a stiff drink, followed by a tasty meal that had miraculously appeared in the kitchen.

As it was, she stood in the kitchen and wearily contemplated the fridge, knowing that if she stopped she would never be able to get going again. If only she hadn't taken such a stand about ready-made meals. This was one time when she could really have done with taking something out of the freezer and heating it up, and to hell with nutritional value. But she seemed to be such a failure as a parent in other ways that sometimes it seemed that the only thing she *could* do for Toby was to make sure that he ate properly.

It looked as if it was going to be pasta again. Drearily, Georgia reached for a couple of tomatoes. She could make a sauce. Toby would groan when he saw it. He was sick of her pasta sauce, which was admittedly not very interesting, but at least it was made with fresh vegetables and would be good for him.

She was just chopping an onion when the doorbell rang. Her eyes were watering from the onion fumes and, without thinking, she took the knife with her to answer the door. She hoped it wasn't someone doing market research or in her current mood she might be tempted to be very rude.

But it wasn't anyone with a clipboard. It was Mac, holding a box.

'Mac!' Even now, with a hammering headache and her eyes streaming from the onions and her spirits at an all time low, the sight of him was enough to make the breath snare in her throat.

'It looks like I've come at a bad time,' said Mac, eyeing the knife in her hand cautiously. 'Er…should I be nervous about the way you're holding that knife?'

'What?' Georgia looked down at the knife. 'Oh.' She wiped the tears from her eyes with the back of her hand. 'No, it's been a bad day, but not that bad,' she said. 'I was just chopping onions.'

'I hope that means you haven't had supper yet?'

'No, I've just got back.'

'What are you making?'

'Pasta and tomato sauce,' said Georgia, puzzled by his sudden interest in her supper menu until it dawned on her that he might be angling for an invitation to eat with them. It seemed a little odd under the circumstances, but then Mac had never been embarrassed about asking for what he wanted.

Now she was going to have to say no, and she hated doing that. Along with just about every other woman she knew, Georgia had been brought up to oblige when people asked her to do things.

It wasn't that she didn't know that she was perfectly entitled to say no if she wanted, but the fact was that she wasn't nearly as assertive as she looked, and refusing politely still went against the grain.

Perhaps she should just get in first?

'Um… I'd like to ask you to join us, but actually it's not a very good time -' she began.

'I was wondering how you'd feel about a curry,' Mac interrupted her, throwing her completely.

'A curry?' She looked at him blankly.

'I've just been to see a mate of mine in Bradford,' he told her. 'Atif? Do you remember him?'

Georgia had the disorientating feeling that she'd somehow missed a few steps in the conversation. What was Mac doing, standing on her doorstep and talking about curries and old friends? *Did* she remember Atif? Georgia wasn't sure about anything any more.

'Er…'

'He's taken over his father's restaurant,' Mac went on, as if this were a perfectly normal conversation to be having when the last time they had talked it had seemed as if their relationship was finally at an end. 'It's one of the best Indian restaurants in the country, and they're doing really well.'

'Oh…well, good…' said Georgia feebly.

'Atif gave me some paste and instructions on how to make it up into a curry. He put some side dishes in, too.'

'Ri-ight,' she said, still unsure where all this was leading.

'The thing is,' said Mac with the air of one taking the plunge, 'I thought you were looking a bit frazzled today, and I remembered what you'd said about longing for a good curry and... Well, I thought maybe I could cook one for you.'

He was making a mess of it, thought Mac glumly. He was so stupidly nervous that he had rushed it. No wonder Georgia was looking as if she had no idea what he was talking about.

As well she might, after his last spectacular failure. Mac hadn't understood at the time, but he had got the message about the Peru trip loud and clear: he had bungled it in a big way.

Simply baffled at first, he had run through a whole range of emotions after Georgia had finished her coffee, thanked him with cool politeness and left that day. Humiliation, anger, bitterness, disappointment and depression had succeeded each other in quick succession. He had spent some time telling himself that she was contrary and unreasonable and that if she was going to shift the goalposts he might as well give up altogether.

And then, finally, he had started to think about what she had said.

'You could have a drink, a bath or something while I make it,' he pushed on with a kind of desperation before Georgia could say no. 'I've got all the stuff here, and Atif gave me step-by-step instructions. I think it should be good.' He waved the box under her nose. 'It smells good already.'

Georgia was looking bemused, and she still hadn't said anything. God, what did she want, for him to go down on his knees?

'So...what do you say?' he asked, hoping he didn't sound too anxious.

'It sounds wonderful, Mac. Really.' Georgia found her voice at last. 'But I'm not sure Toby would enjoy curry.'

Mac had thought of that, and produced his trump card. 'I brought him a pizza,' he said and she lifted an eyebrow.

'Sounds like you were pretty confident that we wouldn't have got round to eating yet!'

'I just *hoped* you wouldn't have,' said Mac quickly. 'I did think about ringing you to let you know that I was coming, but I was afraid that you might say no,' he confessed disarmingly. 'And I've got to admit that I wanted to surprise you, too!'

'You've certainly done that,' said Georgia.

Mac hesitated, then opted for straightness. 'Look, Georgia, I know I got it wrong before,' he said, feeling his way carefully. 'I can see that I made a mistake, thinking that you could drop everything and come to Peru with me, but I've been thinking about what you said, and I want another shot at proving that I really do love you.' He risked a smile. 'I've still got that bet to win, after all!'

Georgia's lungs had suddenly forgotten how to work properly, and were getting all confused about whether they should be inflating or deflating. 'I thought you'd given up on that,' she managed, struggling to find a breath in the middle of it all.

'You know me, Georgia,' he said, the blue eyes brilliant. 'I never give up.'

Georgia swallowed. 'Oh,' was all she could think of to say. See, it was great to have a reputation as an intelligent and impressively articulate journalist.

'So this is me trying again,' said Mac carefully. 'I looked at you today while you were too busy to even notice whether I was there or not, and I thought you seemed tired. I tried to think about what you would most need right now, and I wondered if you might like not to have to think about food for once, if you might like a bit of looking after yourself for a change.'

He paused, the blue gaze still searching her face. 'Is that what you meant when you sent me away to think about what you really needed?'

To her horror, Georgia felt tears prickle her eyes. 'That kind of thing, yes,' she said huskily.

'So will you let me come in and cook this curry for you?'

'Mac, it's a really thoughtful idea, and I do appreciate it, but Toby hasn't had a good day and I'm not sure how he'd feel about—'

'Hello.' Toby's voice from the stairs above her broke into her excuses to Mac and made her swing round in surprise. 'I saw your bike,' he told Mac. 'Have you brought that funny camera?'

Somewhat constrained by the box that he was holding between his hands, Mac lifted an elbow awkwardly to show Toby the camera slung over his shoulder. 'I never go anywhere without it,' he said.

'Can you teach me how to use it again?' asked Toby, starting down the stairs.

'Of course, if that's what you'd like.'

'I would,' said Toby as he arrived at the bottom step. He looked at Mac, standing outside the front door with the box in his hands. 'Are you coming to supper?'

Mac's eyes met Georgia's. Knowing that there was no point in fighting it any further, she stepped back wordlessly and gestured him inside with her knife.

Mac smiled as he walked past her. 'I'm making supper,' he told Toby cheerfully.

It was a very odd feeling when dreams actually came true, thought Georgia as she lay back in the bath, sipping a glass of wine and remembering how she had been longing for just this to happen only a matter of minutes ago, before Mac rang the doorbell and changed everything. Again.

She had left Toby allegedly showing Mac around the kitchen, although she thought privately that his knowledge of where everything lived was more than a little hazy. Still, it wasn't a big kitchen and Mac would just keep looking until he found what he needed. The main thing was that Toby seemed happier, and now the enticing smell of cooking spices was drifting up the stairs.

As she sank luxuriously beneath the bubbles, Georgia found herself wishing that Mac would drift up the stairs too, and wash her back the way he used to. He had wonderful hands, warm and capable with long, deft fingers, and there had been many occasions when he had massaged away the knots of tension in her shoulders. She would lean back into his probing fingers and let herself relax until, imperceptibly, the feel of his hands on her body became less comforting, and more exciting...

Georgia stretched and shivered at the memory. Yes, if Mac would only come upstairs, and then afterwards he could put his arms around her and tell her that everything would be all right... All her fantasies really *would* have come true then!

No, hang on, that wasn't right! Belatedly realising where her thoughts were leading, Georgia sat up so abruptly that the water slopped over the edge of the bath on to the floor.

Mac might be fulfilling her culinary fantasies tonight, but that was as far as she would let her imagination go. She didn't need her back washed, and she didn't need to be held and comforted. She was stronger than that now…*remember*?

She would be foolish indeed to fall back into the old trap of needing Mac just because he had thought about her tonight. It was an encouraging sign, of course, but it would take more than a curry to make her rethink her decision about their divorce. If he really wanted to prove that he loved her, Mac would need to show that he could think about her all the time, not just as a one-off because his pride was hurt by her rejection of the Macchu Pichu trip.

Keep a sense of perspective, Georgia, she told herself sternly. It was wonderful to lie in the bath like this, wonderful to have supper cooked for her, but after all it was just tonight. She couldn't allow herself to believe that she could rely on Mac to think about her like this all the time.

Not yet, anyway.

Mac looked up from the camera as Georgia came into the living room and his heart skipped a beat. She had undone her hair the way he liked it and it fell loosely to her shoulders, still slightly damp from the bath. She was wearing loose grey yoga pants and a white long-sleeved T-shirt, and she looked easily ten years younger than the woman who had opened the door earlier.

'You look better,' he said, his voice just slightly off-key, and he lifted the camera to take a picture of her to cover his ridiculous confusion.

'I feel better,' said Georgia frankly, feeling unaccountably shy once again. She looked around the living room, touched to see that the table had already been laid. 'Is there anything I can do? Do you want me to have a look at what's going on in the kitchen?'

'No!' Mac got to his feet hurriedly. 'No, don't go in there. It's all ready, anyway. You sit down and I'll bring it out.'

'I've got pizza,' Toby told Georgia importantly as he pulled out his chair. 'Mac got me Pizza Margarita. That's my favourite.'

'That was clever of him to guess that,' said Georgia, sitting obediently at the table and more relieved than she wanted to admit to see that Toby's sullen mood had vanished.

'I helped him make the curry, too. He's going to show me how the camera works again after supper.'

Mac had clearly found a way under Toby's guard. Georgia wasn't sure quite how he had done it, but Toby was more animated than she had ever seen him. She watched his small face light up as he chatted away to Mac about computer games and the camera, and for the first time she saw him less as Becca's child and more as an individual, with his own interests, however baffling and technological they might be to her.

While she was grateful to Mac for helping Toby to open up, a little bit of Georgia couldn't help feeling resentful that he had got through to the little boy so easily when she herself had had to spend months trying to gain his trust.

She felt ashamed, too, that she hadn't noticed what it was that really interested Toby before. It was such hard work just getting through the day sometimes that she hadn't taken the time to look at him and really *see* him, the way she had wanted Mac to see her when they were married.

Torn by conflicting feelings, Georgia insisted on doing the washing up while the two of them talked cameras. She needed a little time on her own, although she nearly changed her mind when she saw the kitchen. No wonder Mac hadn't wanted her to go in there! The mess he and Toby had created was truly spectacular.

Still, the curry had been so good and she was so glad to see Toby talking again that Georgia pulled on some rubber gloves and got on with it. She cleared up absently, wondering if she should try and ask him again what had been wrong earlier, but it seemed a shame to remind him of his problem—whatever it was—and spoil the happy atmosphere.

If only she felt more confident with him.

Georgia rinsed the plates before stacking the dishwasher carefully. Was it easier to deal with your own child? she wondered. Did parents know instinctively what to say and to do, or was everyone bumbling along and making the same mistakes she did?

It took a long time to restore the kitchen to some semblance of order and, when Georgia finally made it back to the sitting room, Mac's expression of trepidation was so comical that she couldn't help laughing. 'I suppose you *had* to use every single utensil in the kitchen?' she pretended to scold him.

'I had to,' he agreed. 'I thought some things were looking a bit dusty, and I knew that way they'd all get a good clean!'

Toby looked up from the camera, uninterested in domestic details. 'Can I have a camera for my birthday?' he asked Georgia. 'Not a digital camera, one just like this?'

A mental price tag of hundreds of pounds flashed before Georgia's eyes. She knew how much Mac's cameras cost. 'I think that camera is a little bit complicated for you at the moment, isn't it?' she suggested, but Toby was stung.

'It isn't! I know how to use it, don't I, Mac?'

'I think a smaller camera would be better for you to practise on,' said Mac tactfully. 'I can show Georgia some suitable models if you like.'

Toby frowned. 'Will you make sure she gets the right one?'

'I'll do my best,' he promised solemnly.

Georgia felt like pointing out that she was more than capable of choosing a suitable camera herself, but there was no point in resisting male solidarity. 'It's not your birthday yet,' she said instead. 'You might change your mind about what you want before then.'

'I won't.' Toby looked so intense that her heart twisted. 'Honest.'

'Well, let's see how good you are, shall we?' she said lightly. 'On which note, I think it's time for you to go to bed.'

Toby automatically opened his mouth to argue, and then thought better of it. 'OK,' he said, with such an angelic look and such transparent motives that Georgia and Mac couldn't help laughing.

He trailed off towards the stairs, but stopped and turned at the door as a thought struck him.

'If you're still married,' he said, 'can Mac come and live with us?'

CHAPTER EIGHT

GEORGIA gave a gasp of embarrassment, which was followed by a ghastly silence. Ghastly from her point of view, anyway. Mac was, as always, totally unfazed, but a grin was tugging at the corner of his mouth.

'Toby, we're not really married,' she managed.

'But Mac said he was your husband,' Toby pointed out, all reasonableness.

'Well, yes, and he *is*, technically,' Georgia floundered.

She had been hoping that Toby had forgotten that conversation he had overhead the first night that Mac had turned up. He had never mentioned it again, so she hadn't thought it was worth confusing him with a long-winded explanation of how Mac came to be her husband without apparently figuring in her life at all.

It was all Mac's fault. She had introduced him to Toby as an old friend, so he had known perfectly well that she hadn't wanted him to know about their marriage, but no, he had had to drop 'husband' into the conversation! He had only done it to wind up Geoffrey. And now, when she needed his help in trying to make Toby understand their unconventional relationship, all he could do was stand there looking amused.

It looked as if it was up to her to deal with the explanations. Nothing new there, then.

'The thing is, Toby, Mac and I aren't properly married,' she ploughed on, glaring at Mac, who wasn't helping at *all*. 'At least, not in the sense that we live together. It's...well, it's complicated.' She sighed, giving up. How could she possibly explain her relationship with Mac to a small boy?

Toby wasn't interested in complicated. 'Because you could have the spare bed in my room, if you wanted,' he said generously to Mac.

'That's kind, Toby,' said Mac, poker-faced. 'But you know, I've got somewhere very comfortable to live at the moment. I'll probably just stay there for now.'

'Oh. OK.' Toby looked disappointed but appeared to accept this as a reasonable excuse for Mac not moving in. 'When can you show me the camera again?'

'We could go out on Saturday,' said Mac. 'I'll show you how to use the light meter. You could be my assistant.'

The expression on Toby's face gave Georgia a pang. 'Cool,' he breathed and drifted happily upstairs.

Still weak with relief that Mac hadn't taken the opportunity to move in—and she wouldn't have put it past him!—Georgia followed him and, by the time she came downstairs again, she had recovered some of her composure.

'Thank you for being so kind to Toby,' she said. 'He's thrilled at the idea of going out with you on Saturday. I hope it won't be too boring for you.'

'I won't be bored,' said Mac, who was sitting in one of the armchairs and looking utterly at home. 'He's a good kid. I like him. He's obviously very intelligent too.'

He studied Georgia's face as she curled up in the corner of the sofa in an unconsciously defensive posture. She looked tired again, if not as tense as before. 'I can see he's not an easy child, though,' he added.

'No,' said Georgia with feeling, thinking of the past year, of how she had struggled to establish a bond with Toby. 'It's been hard, but I think it's getting better as we get more used to each other.'

'No regrets then?'

'About taking Toby?' She shook her head, and the hair which had dried in soft waves, gleamed in the lamplight. It was still the same beautiful pale gold that Mac remembered and he longed to be able to reach out and touch it, to rub it between his fingers and tangle his fingers in the silken strands again.

'No,' Georgia was answering his question, although Mac himself was distracted. 'At least... Well, if I'm honest, when I'm tired I think about my old life in London, and I do sometimes wish that I could have it back,' she said. 'But only in the same way that I wish Becca hadn't died,' she added quickly. 'Not because I don't want Toby.'

'That's understandable,' said Mac, forcing himself to concentrate on what she was saying and not on the curve of her body, the shape of her mouth, the sweep of her lashes, the proud tilt of her head.

'When I feel like that, I think about how it would have been for Toby if I had let him be taken into care,' said Georgia, relieved that Mac seemed quite happy to stick to a neutral topic. 'What would it be like for a little boy of seven to feel that there was no one who wanted him? I can't bear that thought. I'm not saying I don't get tired and fed up and frustrated, because I do, and Toby can be really difficult sometimes, but...he's lost his mother, he never had a father, he hasn't got anything.'

'He's got you,' said Mac.

Georgia sighed and ran her fingers through her hair in a distracted gesture that made Mac's whole body clench with desire.

'I'm not his mother, though,' she said. 'I feel so useless most of the time, and if I'm not feeling inadequate, I'm terrified by all the responsibility!

I just flounder around, trying to do the right thing for Toby, but getting it wrong most of the time.'

She had tried to keep her voice light and self-deprecating, but Mac could tell how much it bothered her. Georgia didn't like not being good at things, and bringing up a child would be uncharted territory for her.

'You're not getting it wrong,' he said reassuringly. 'Toby seems fine to me. I think you should relax. You're being yourself and doing the best you can. You can't do more than that.'

Reaching over, he refilled the glass which she had put on the small table beside her. 'I always thought you'd be a good mother, and you are, but Toby needs a father too.'

'And I suppose you think the job should be yours?'

Mac hesitated. 'He did ask me to move in,' he reminded her.

'He likes you, that's obvious,' said Georgia slowly. 'Toby doesn't take to many people, so that's a big thing, but…' she trailed off, wondering how to put her reservations into words. '…but please be careful, Mac,' she went on after a moment. 'If Toby comes to rely on you and then you disappear, he'll be hurt. Don't let him put his hopes on you and then disappoint him. I don't want him to have to go through that.'

Mac made an impatient movement. 'I'm not going to disappear!'

'You don't exactly have a track record of staying put,' Georgia pointed out. 'How long were we married?'

She didn't really mean it as a question, but Mac answered anyway.

'Nine years and four months.'

Faint colour touched Georgia's cheekbones at the evidence of how well he remembered their marriage, and her eyes slid away from his. She mustn't get diverted.

'And during those nine years, how many months did you spend in one place?' she asked him. 'Even when we had a base, like in Africa or London, you were always away on assignments.'

'That's just a question of geography,' said Mac dismissively. 'We may have been physically apart, but emotionally there wasn't any distance. Surely what matters is that I was faithful to you. I never looked at another woman in all that time,' he told her, irritation creeping into his voice at last. 'Don't tell me I haven't got staying power!'

'It's different for a child. If Toby came to think of you as his father, he'd need you to be there, and stay there. It's all very well for you to say that you would stay around, but I know you. You get bored, and then you're off looking for the next thing.'

'I'm not bored at the moment.'

'You've only been here a few weeks,' said Georgia, unimpressed. 'I can't imagine you still

being happy to photograph lollipop ladies and
school hockey teams in a year's time, let alone in
five years—in *ten* years—and that's how long
Toby needs his father figure to stick around. He
needs someone who's always going to be there,
not just as long as he's having a good time.'

Mac hadn't taken his eyes off her face, and she
was desperately conscious of his intent blue gaze.
Shifting on the sofa, she moistened her lips sur-
reptitiously.

If only he wouldn't sit there like that, looking
lean and rangy and at ease in his own skin, with
that mouth and that jaw and those eyes that made
her itch and tingle with longing to throw caution
to the wind, to give in and say that of *course* he
could stay, of course he could move back into her
life and her heart if only he would take her in his
arms and make love to her the way he used to.

If she would just give in, she could go over to
where he sat and let him pull her down on to his
lap. His arms would close around her and he
would smile that smile that melted her bones, and
then he would kiss her, and oh, it would be so
good…

Georgia's breath shortened. She could practically taste his lips, almost feel his hands hard and
warm against her, sliding deliciously over her
skin while desire pulsed dark and dangerous deep
inside her.

If she gave in, she could burrow into his

strength, spread her hands over his lean, powerful body, kiss her way along his jaw to his mouth. She would be able to touch him and taste him and feel him the way she had longed to do for four long years.

It would be so easy. He wanted her, and he was just there, only a few feet away... She wouldn't have to say a word. Georgia's pulse roared in her ears and the temptation to get up and go over to him was so strong that she felt giddy with it. Only sheer force of will was keeping her on the sofa.

Force of will and the memory of how much it had hurt when things had fallen apart before.

'I know Toby likes you,' she said with difficulty. 'You're right when you say he's going to need a father. I know you're fun to be around but, in the long run, I think he'd be better off with someone like Geoffrey as a role model.'

'Geoffrey!' Mac snorted contemptuously. 'What makes him such a great role model?'

'He's a good man,' said Georgia quietly. 'He'll care for me and care for Toby, and he won't let either of us down.'

'I wouldn't let you down either!'

'It's going to take more than a curry to convince me of that, Mac. We're talking about my life here, my life and Toby's life. I don't want him to learn about disappointment and heartache until he has to. He's had enough upheaval in his life.'

She made herself meet Mac's eyes. 'There's no way I'm going to gamble throwing my lot in with someone so important to his happiness until I'm absolutely sure it's the right thing to do,' she told him. 'I might take the risk for myself,' she said, thinking of her clamouring body, 'but I'm not doing it for Toby.'

'Then I'm just going to have to keep on trying until you trust me,' said Mac.

Georgia chewed her bottom lip. 'It would be easier if you gave up.'

'Easier for you, or easier for me?'

'For us both.'

Mac shook his head. 'Sorry,' he said, 'I'm not prepared to do that.'

He got up to leave and Georgia saw him to the door, not knowing what else she could say to convince him. She waited until he had shrugged on his jacket and hoisted the motorcycle helmet in one hand.

'Thank you for tonight, Mac,' she said, but her throat felt absurdly tight suddenly, as if she wanted to cry, but wasn't sure why. 'It was a great curry.'

'My pleasure.'

Mac reached out and took her chin in his free hand. His long, strong fingers seemed to burn into her skin, but he held her lightly so that she could easily pull away if she wanted to, but something held her, something that made her heart slam against her ribcage and interfered with her breathing. When she didn't move, just stood there and gazed dumbly back at him with her great, smoky-grey eyes, Mac bent his head and touched his lips to hers in a very gentle kiss.

'I'm not giving up, Georgia,' he said softly as he dropped his hand and her knees gave such a fine impression of cotton wool that she had to fall back against the hall wall for support. 'As far as I'm concerned, the bet's still on.'

He's here!' Toby had been stationed at the window all morning, waiting for Mac.

He ran to open the front door, while Georgia smoothed her hands down her skirt and tried to rearrange her face into a composed expression befitting a forty-one-year-old professional in full control of her life, who knew exactly what she wanted and how to get it.

As opposed to a middle-aged woman in a complete muddle about everything, which was how she really felt.

It was ridiculous, but her lips were still tingling and throbbing as if seared by that last gentle kiss. Georgia couldn't help feeling that she was too old to be carrying on like this, but look at her, endlessly replaying her conversation with Mac like a teenager! It wasn't dignified. Thank goodness she had resisted the impulse to ring her best friend in London and subject her to a long and tedious account of what *he* had said, and what *she* had said, with an in-depth analysis of what each of them had actually meant.

There was no need for analysis, Georgia told herself sternly. She had been as clear as she could. She had been straight with Mac; she had told him to give up.

The worst thing was that every time she thought of the way he had told her that he wasn't going to do that, she got a squirmy feeling at the base of her spine.

Georgia was unable to find a good excuse for her own perversity. Over and over again, her head reassured her that she had made the right decision, while her weak and treacherous body kept coming up with ridiculous fantasies which involved succumbing to the temptation of falling into his arms while simultaneously managing in some unspecified way to hold on to her pride and avoid any risk to her heart.

Not that she had had much opportunity to succumb recently, Georgia thought somewhat sourly. For someone so confident of his ability to convince her of his commitment, Mac was doing a remarkably good job of ignoring her again. She had hardly seen him for the past two days, and was annoyed with herself for feeling a sense of anticipation this morning at the thought that she would at least see him when he came to pick up Toby.

And now here he was. Taking a deep breath, Georgia went to greet him where he was still standing on the doorstep, his head cocked to one side as he listened to Toby chattering.

'Hello,' she said. Her heart was thumping uncomfortably but she achieved a cool smile. At least, she hoped it was cool. 'Has Toby asked if you'd like to come in?'

Mac looked up at the sound of her voice, and the expression that blazed briefly in his eyes made her shiver inside. Or was it just the sight of him— the tantalising quirk of his mouth, the crease in his cheek, the humour in his face?

'I think we might as well head straight off,' he said. 'That is if you're ready, Toby? Have you got a jacket?'

Inevitably, Toby turned to Georgia. 'Where's my jacket, Georgia?'

'On the hook by the back door, where it always is,' said Georgia, resigned. She watched as Toby ran back to the kitchen, then made herself meet Mac's eyes once more, but that disturbing look had vanished so completely that she wondered if she had imagined it.

That thought left her worryingly disappointed, so she put on her best smile and took refuge in small talk. 'Where are you going?'

'I thought we'd go out on to the moors.'

'The moors?' Georgia was startled out of her carefully cool composure. 'Surely you're not thinking of taking Toby on that bike of yours? It's much too dangerous!'

Mac rolled his eyes. 'Of course not!' He gestured grandly towards the road, where an estate car was parked behind Georgia's own smart black hatchback. 'I'm now the proud owner of a sensible family car,' he told her. 'I'm sure even Geoffrey would approve!'

'You've *bought* a car?' Georgia stared at it. It was bright red but otherwise so unremarkable that it was hard to imagine Mac driving it, let alone buying it.

'Yes. What do you think?'

Georgia didn't know *what* to think. Part of her was pleased, flattered even. Buying a car like that was surely a sign that Mac had matured, and was ready to settle down and be sensible. That part wanted to believe that he had done it for her.

But she was conscious, too, of a pang of regret. Mac had always had a motorbike, even in Africa. She remembered sitting behind him, her arms around his waist, and feeling safe and thrilled at the same time. There was something about the hot wind on her face, something about the country rushing past while she and Mac were still and steady, pressed tightly together on the bike, leaning as one into the bends in the road.

The bike had been part of being young, being *alive*, unshackled by responsibilities or desires beyond living every glorious moment. It meant freedom and fun and being able to weave through traffic jams and leave everyone else stuck in their oh-so-sensible cars while the open road beckoned.

It was part of what made Mac the man he was—reckless, unconventional, even irresponsible sometimes—but still a man who knew how to enjoy life more than anyone else Georgia had ever known.

'Are you sure you know what you're doing?' she said. 'Driving a car is a bit different from a bike.'

'Surely you're not giving me advice about driving?' said Mac, amused. 'You'll be telling me how to cook next!'

She put up her chin. 'I'm just concerned about Toby,' she said, refusing to rise to the bait.

'Don't worry about him. He'll be fine, and I'll drive carefully, I promise. I'm going to teach him about photographing landscapes. The light will be great on the moors today.'

Georgia imagined the two of them up in the hills. It was a bright, blustery April day and it would be exhilarating up there in the heather, with only the wind and the open skyline for company.

'It sounds lovely,' she said wistfully, wishing that she could go too. It was a bit much when you were envious of your own nephew's date.

Maybe Mac would ask her if she wanted to go along. If he was serious about wanting to spend the rest of his life with her, a morning together on the moors would be a good place to start, wouldn't it?

'Yes, it should be good,' said Mac, ignoring his cue. 'What are you doing today?'

Not going to the moors, obviously.

'Oh, just catching up on a few jobs,' said Georgia, not sure whether to be relieved or miffed that he hadn't picked up on her blatant fishing for an invitation.

She hadn't actually thought beyond how it would feel to see Mac again, so she would need to invent some jobs pretty smartish. 'I bought a storage unit for Toby's room so that he's got somewhere to put all his stuff—apart from the carpet, that is—so I could finish putting that together.'

It was as good a plan as any.

'I'm surprised Geoffrey's not doing that for you,' said Mac. 'I thought he was your handyman of choice?'

'I'm quite capable of doing it myself,' she said with something of a snap.

She had, in fact, mentioned the fact that the unit was self-assembly to Geoffrey, who had sighed as he'd pulled out his diary.

'I don't know when I'll be able to come round and put it together for you,' he had said fretfully. 'This project is taking up so much time at the moment…'

Georgia had been so irritated by the implication

that she couldn't possibly manage to do it herself
that she had stomped home, determined to put that
unit together on her own if it killed her. So far
she had managed to construct an alarmingly wob-
bly frame and one a drawer upside down, and had
ended up so frustrated that one cross kick had
been sufficient to make it all fall apart, which was
how it had remained.

So today she could tackle the impenetrable di-
agrams again. She was a perfectly intelligent, capable woman and she had her own screwdriver.
If all those men could put stupid bits of furniture
together, so could she. A nice quiet day was all
she needed.

'She said *really* bad words last time she tried
to make that thing,' Toby confided in Mac. He
had found his jacket and was dragging it by the
sleeve, the rest of it trailing along the ground.
'She was really cross!'

Mac laughed as Georgia flushed, and his blue
eyes danced. 'Sure you don't want a hand?' he
asked her.

'No, thank you,' she said with dignity. 'I'll be
fine on my own.'

Brave words, but she regretted them almost as
soon as she had squared up to the pieces of the
unit spread over Toby's bedroom floor. The dia-
grams made even less sense this time round, and
it wasn't long before Georgia was thoroughly
confused. The more confused she got, the angrier

and more humiliated she felt, and the less able to tackle the whole thing logically. In the end, she had to unpick everything and, thoroughly fed up, hide the pieces in her bedroom.

At least Toby was spared the language this time.

Mac brought him back later that afternoon.

'Did you have a good time?' Georgia asked him, although she hardly needed to ask. He had obviously loved it.

'Brilliant!' said Toby, his eyes shining. 'We're going again next Saturday.'

Having carefully not looked directly at Mac, Georgia found herself glancing at him to check that this wasn't merely wishful thinking on Toby's part.

'If that's OK with you,' he said. 'We've already planned the next stage of our photography course, haven't we, Toby?' He clapped the little boy on the shoulder. 'Toby's got a real feel for a camera,' he said, and Georgia could see Toby glowing with pride.

'It looks like I'll be getting you a camera for your birthday after all,' she said lightly to cover the sudden clutch at her heart.

Toby's face lit up. 'Oh, yes, *please*, Georgia!'

Mac laughed at his heartfelt expression. 'How did you get on with that unit you were building?' he asked, turning to Georgia.

'Oh...that. Fine. All done,' she lied brightly

and hastened to change the subject. 'What about
a cup of tea? I've got scones, but you'll be glad
to know that I didn't try to make them myself!'

Mac glanced at his watch. 'That sounds good,
but I'd better not. I'm meeting some friends for
a drink later, and I've a few things to do before
then. Thanks, anyway.'

Fine. It wasn't that she *wanted* him to stay for
a while, but it would obviously have been rude
not to invite him in after he had had Toby all day.
If he didn't want to come in, that was perfectly
OK with her, thought Georgia huffily.

Go and meet your precious friends, she wanted
to shout childishly after him as he headed back to
his sensible new car. See if I care!

She didn't, of course, because that wouldn't be
dignified. She just let Toby walk past her, still
talking about f-stops and shutter speeds, and followed him inside, relieving her feelings by shut-
ting the front door behind her with a bang.

Georgia stood next to Rose's desk, flicking absently through the post that had arrived that morning while Cassie tried to convince her that what
the *Gazette* needed now was a special leisure supplement.

'A pull-out supplement would be very expensive to produce,' said Georgia. 'I like it as a con-
cept, though. Oh, look at this!' She broke off,

riffling through a glossy brochure. 'It's for that new spa on the Pickering road.'

'In the old castle?' Rose peered to look.

'Yes, doesn't it look fabulous?' Georgia turned the brochure round so that Cassie could see the photographs of a gleaming pool surrounded by tropical plants, exquisitely decorated bedrooms and women undergoing a range of exotic treatments. 'A mud wrap—how would you fancy one of those?'

Cassie looked interested. 'They say it does wonderful things for your skin,' she said. 'It's supposed to get rid of all the dead cells.'

The conversation diverted briefly into a discussion about skin products and the relative merits of massage or a make-up session, moved on to whether a pedicure would make you feel better than a new pair of shoes—this clearly depended on the shoes—and thence to their own preferences on the retail therapy front, before returning to the spa via a heated debate about the dress style of a certain well-known film star and whether they would personally want to be married to her gorgeous but notoriously philandering husband.

It was the kind of exclusively female conversation that Georgia had used to have with her friends in London, and she hadn't realised how much she had missed it until then. It was amazing how a few minutes' chat about trivia could make you feel better, so that you simply didn't care about the looks Mac and Kevin were exchanging. If they couldn't keep up with the rapid shifts in the conversation they were blatantly eavesdropping on, that was their problem!

Georgia finally brought them back to the matter in hand. 'Well, Cassie, if you fancy being smeared with mud and having seaweed slapped all over you before being wrapped in cling film, here's your chance,' she said, having discovered the letter that had accompanied the brochure while the other two were still gasping over the eye-popping prices.

'They're offering a free day of luxury pampering for the Features Editor,' she said, waving the letter. 'And, in the absence of anyone else, I'd say that was you, Cassie. I don't see why we shouldn't write a piece about the new local spa as part of our new leisure section, and *obviously* you'll need to go and try all the treatments! Not that I think I'd bother with the mud and the seaweed if it was me,' she said, gazing longingly at the brochure. 'It would be bliss just to lie on one of those beds by the pool and sleep for a day!'

'Do I need to go straight away?' asked Cassie.

Georgia consulted the letter. 'The offer's only open until next Monday.' She made a face. 'Seems a bit restrictive. Either they want us to write about them or they don't.'

'Oh, well,' said Cassie vaguely, 'I expect they

have to limit these things somehow. The trouble is, I don't think I'll be able to make it. I'm busy.'

'What, all weekend?'

'Afraid so.'

'Oh.' Georgia was a little puzzled by Cassie's lack of enthusiasm after their earlier conversation. 'Oh, well, that's a shame. What about you, Rose? Do you fancy trying your hand at writing an article?'

'I don't think I'd be able to write anything,' said Rose. 'And my daughter's coming this weekend.'

'What about Meredith?' Georgia called her over from her desk and showed her the brochure.

'It's not really my kind of thing,' said Meredith.

'*Someone* must be able to go!' said Georgia, frustrated.

'What about you?' said Rose. 'You never take up any perks, and you were just saying how much you'd love to spend a day there.'

'I would, but I haven't got time to go in the week, and I don't like to leave Toby at the weekend.'

'I thought Mac said he was teaching Toby how to take photographs?' said Cassie and, before Georgia could object, she had called Mac over.

'Hey, Mac, we were just telling Georgia she should take up the offer of a free day at this spa at the weekend. You'll have Toby, won't you?'

'On Saturday,' said Mac, taking the brochure from Cassie and flicking through it. 'Not sure it's your kind of thing, though, Georgia. It looks a bit self-indulgent for you. You'd never be able to relax enough to enjoy it.'

'Yes, I would.' Georgia snatched the brochure back from him. 'I can relax as well as *anyone*. I'll spend all Saturday there, and I can assure you that I will enjoy every minute of it!'

She marched off to ring the spa, determined to prove to Mac that she was perfectly capable of self-indulgence on a grand scale.

By the time Saturday came round, Georgia was feeling less confident of her ability to relax. She had been so busy all week that she hadn't had a chance to clean the house properly, and everything was a mess. She hated it like that.

The truth was that she would rather spend the time on her own putting the house back in order than waste the day at a spa, and only the thought of Mac's reaction if she didn't go stopped her ringing up and cancelling. She didn't want another lecture from him about how uptight she was. She would relax today if it killed her.

And, in fact, as soon as she walked through the doors of the spa Georgia felt the tension start to unravel. Everything was so calm and quiet and clean, it was like being transported to another world, to a parallel universe of hushed luxury, where there were no ringing phones and no mess, no responsibilities and no deadlines to meet. Where she had nothing to do but to lie back and be pampered.

Georgia gave herself up to the sheer luxury of it all and let herself be steamed and scrubbed and slathered with lotions, and after a while she even stopped thinking. By the end of the day she was so relaxed that it was an effort to stand upright. She hadn't realised quite how wound-up she had been until she felt how easily she could flex her shoulders now.

'This is a wonderful place,' she said to the girl on reception when she went to collect her keys. 'I'm going to be writing such a rave article you'll be inundated!'

The girl looked alarmed at the prospect. 'Article?' she said warily.

'I'm from the *Askerby and District Gazette*,' Georgia explained. 'I presumed you offered a free day here so that we could publicise the spa?'

'Absolutely not.' The girl shook her head firmly. 'We offer such an exclusive experience that we don't need to advertise, and we're very strict about not offering freebies for PR purposes. Someone must have bought your voucher.'

'No, honestly, it came to the paper,' said Georgia, digging in her bag for it. 'Look.' She handed over the voucher.

The girl inspected it and then started tapping at the keyboard, watching the computer screen with a slight frown. 'Ah, no, it's as I thought,' she said, her face lightening at last. 'Our records say that your voucher was purchased by a Mr M Henderson. Does that mean anything to you?'

'Yes,' said Georgia. 'It does.'

CHAPTER NINE

Georgia drove home in a thoughtful mood. Mac had gone to a lot of trouble to make sure that she had a relaxing day.

It was all falling into place now. He had obviously charmed the manageress at the spa into sending the letter, and primed Cassie and Rose and even Meredith to turn down the chance if she offered it to them. No wonder they had all looked so vague! Georgia didn't know whether to be touched or annoyed at the way they had all fooled her so effectively. To top it all off, Mac had ensured that she would go herself by telling her that she didn't know how to relax. He had known quite well that she would be determined to prove him wrong.

All that effort, and he had done it for her.

A warm, tingling glow was uncurling deep inside her, spreading outwards until it simmered quietly at her fingertips and at the ends of her toes. It might have been the lingering effects of her innovative cling film wrap with mud from the Dead Sea. Or it might have been the knowledge that Mac had really thought about her, and made it impossible for her not to accept the break she needed. It was only now, after a day of enforced rest, that Georgia realised just how badly she had needed it.

But Mac had known.

'Hello!' she called, letting herself in the front door.

No reply. Georgia called again, but the house had that unmistakably empty air to it and she felt stupidly let down. She had been so sure that Mac would be there with Toby, waiting to see how she had enjoyed her day.

Oh, well, she might as well get on with the clearing up while she had the opportunity.

But when Georgia opened the door to the living room, it was immaculate, the floor clear of toys, and everything in place. The kitchen was the same. So tidy was it, that she actually began to wonder if she had in fact cleaned it that morning and somehow wiped the whole event from her memory.

Curious now, she went upstairs. The bathroom was pristine. Her study and bedroom were always neat anyway, so that just left Toby's room. Georgia opened the door, braced for the chaos that reigned in there. She had given up trying to tidy it more than superficially. It was hard enough to hold the line at keeping the living room clear.

She hardly recognized the room when she

opened the door. The unit she had made such a mess of had been put together and secured to the wall, and all of Toby's bits and pieces were stored along the shelves or in the deep drawers. She could even see the carpet. Georgia's throat tightened.

The sound of the front door opening made her turn and, from the top of the stairs, she saw Toby come in with Mac.

'Oh, you're back!' said Toby sounding disappointed as he spotted her. 'We wanted to surprise you.'

'You have surprised me,' said Georgia.

'I helped Mac make up the unit,' said Toby importantly. 'Did you like it?'

'Yes,' she said. 'I liked it a lot.' Over the top of Toby's head, her eyes met Mac's. 'Thank you,' she said simply, but Mac could read her expression, and he nodded.

'We've just been shopping,' he said. 'That's why we weren't here when you arrived. We're making you supper.'

'I think you've both done enough today,' said Georgia.

'No, that's OK. We've planned it all, haven't we, Toby?'

Toby nodded, but Georgia thought his nod was slightly less enthusiastic. He had obviously had enough of being helpful for one day. 'How about you have some time off now, Toby?' she said.

'I'll help Mac with supper as soon as I've got changed.'

Toby didn't wait to be asked twice, and disappeared to his computer.

When Georgia went down to the kitchen, having changed her practical top and trousers for a soft cotton dress that swirled softly around her legs, Mac was busy chopping vegetables. She stood for a moment in the doorway, feeling the familiar clench at the base of her spine as she watched him intent on his task.

As if sensing her gaze, Mac looked up and his eyes warmed. 'You look nice,' he said. 'I thought you'd given up changing for the evening?'

'Oh, well, my other clothes were a bit sticky with all the lotions and potions they slather on you at the spa,' said Georgia, wishing she hadn't felt she needed to explain. She hugged her arms together, feeling nervous suddenly without knowing why. 'What can I do?'

'You can grate some Parmesan if you like.'

Mac handed her the cheese and the grater, and Georgia took them, being careful not to brush her fingers against his. 'Sure you trust me to do this?' she asked, knowing he must have had to think of a job that wouldn't tax her culinary skills too far.

He laughed. 'I expect you can manage that. I didn't want to give you anything too messy in case you spoilt that dress.'

Georgia grated away, keeping her attention

firmly fixed on the cheese, but excruciatingly aware of Mac moving around the kitchen. Under her lashes, she could see him throwing onions into a pan, tossing a tomato in his hand before chopping it in a few deft movements, rubbing his jaw thoughtfully as he considered the recipe. He was all lean lines and powerful muscle, every plane of his body somehow definite so that even the creases at the edges of his eyes stood out with unnatural clarity, and the image of the mobile curve of his mouth lingered long after Georgia had wrenched her gaze away.

After a while the silence began to lengthen uncomfortably. Georgia popped a bit of Parmesan in her mouth and cleared her throat. 'Thank you for today, Mac,' she said.

'Oh, it didn't take long to put that unit together,' he said and stirred the onions casually.

'I meant for all of today,' said Georgia. 'I know it was you that organised the voucher for the spa.'

'Ah.' Mac rested the wooden spoon on the edge of the pan. 'I forgot you were a journalist, and bound to get to the bottom of it in the end!'

'Why did you go to such lengths to keep it a secret?'

He hunched a shoulder. 'I suppose after the Peru fiasco I was nervous that you might be angry with me for trying to organise your life again,' he admitted with just enough embarrassment to make Georgia smile.

'I promise you, I'm not angry about today!'

'Don't tell me I got it right for once!' Mac picked up his knife again, trying to make a joke of it.

'Yes, you got it right,' she said quietly. 'I didn't know how much I needed a break until I had one. Today was perfect. I don't know how to thank you.'

Mac's eyes blazed an intense blue. Putting down his knife, he took the grater from Georgia's hand. 'I think you do,' he said softly.

Very gently, he took hold of her waist, feeling the silky material of her dress slip slightly over her warm, smooth skin as he pulled her towards him, and his whole body clenched with desire.

Mac had a strategy. He had realised the night that he had turned up on the doorstep with curry that nothing was to be gained by rushing Georgia. She was too strong a personality to be jockeyed into anything she didn't want to do, and any suggestion of pushing would just make her dig in her heels.

Very well, Mac had decided, he would treat her like a wary animal that needed to be coaxed into coming closer. He wouldn't crowd her or startle her with sudden gestures that would only make her withdraw. He had deliberately kept his distance since their last kiss, hoping that she would start to trust him at last, and he told himself that if he did get close enough to kiss her again, it would be like last time: gentle, sweet, understanding.

So much for strategy! The moment he touched her, all Mac's fine plans evaporated with the fierceness of his need for her. Jerking Georgia against him, his mouth came down hard on hers, and then they were kissing, hot hungry kisses that ignited the banked up emotion of the last few weeks. The scent and softness and warmth of her made his head reel.

She was so pliant, so responsive in his arms, as desperate as he to hold tighter, to kiss more deeply. Her hands were almost frantic on him, pulling him closer, digging her fingers into his shoulders, and Mac couldn't help himself. Succumbing to the great rolling tide of desire that bore him powerless before it, he backed Georgia almost roughly up against the fridge and kissed his way greedily down her throat while his hand pushed against the dress, sliding over it, slipping down to her knee, and then finding a way beneath the slippery material, pushing it impatiently aside so that he could caress the silken length of her thigh.

It had been too long. He wanted—*needed*—to touch every inch of her, every millimetre, to possess her anew, and when Georgia tipped her head back, arching towards his touch as she gasped his name, Mac felt a surge of exultation. She was still his, still the same, still Georgia…

'Is supper nearly ready?' Toby's clear little voice broke them apart as effectively as a bucket of water, leaving both Mac and Georgia shocked and disorientated.

Instinctively, Mac jerked away from Georgia, who buckled back against the fridge, frantically straightening her dress. Her hair was tousled around her face, her eyes huge and dark, and she looked so desirable that it was all Mac could do not to reach for her again, Toby or no Toby.

It was actually Georgia who recovered first. 'Toby,' she said unsteadily, and swallowed. 'I...we thought you were playing on the computer.'

'It's only that I want to watch that programme about dinosaurs and if supper's late I'll miss it,' Toby explained with the ruthless egocentricity of a child.

'Right, well...it won't be long,' said Georgia who couldn't even remember what they were supposed to be making, let alone what stage they were at.

'OK.' His question answered, Toby turned and went back upstairs, apparently unperturbed by the sight of Mac pressing his aunt up against the refrigerator.

There was a reverberating silence in the kitchen when he had gone. 'Well,' said Mac after a moment, 'we'd better get on.'

No reference was made to the kiss they had

shared, and Georgia was glad of the chance to calm down over supper. Toby seemed unconcerned by catching them *in flagrante*, as it were, and chatted away as normal, but Georgia was mortified. Five minutes later and he might have found her on the floor with Mac. Neither of them had been in a state to think clearly and remember that there was a small boy in the house.

Supper was interminable, and yet it was over too soon. Georgia was unbearably aware of Mac sitting on the other side of the table, talking to Toby as if nothing whatsoever had happened. It didn't look as if *his* heart was still panicking around in his chest the way hers was. He didn't even have the grace to look chastened. Instead he would smile across at her every now and then and, on the few occasions when she found herself unable to avoid his eyes, his expression had been warm and amused more than anything else.

Sure enough, when Georgia could no longer find an excuse to dither upstairs with Toby, Mac smiled broadly and got up off the sofa to hold out his arms. 'Come here,' he said.

'No.' She hadn't meant it to come out quite that abruptly, and Mac's smile blinked off as if she had slapped him.

'*No?* How can you say say no after the way you kissed me out there in the kitchen?' he demanded.

It was a fair point, and Georgia swallowed. 'I

shouldn't have done that, I'm sorry. I think it was being at the spa all day,' she tried to explain. 'I was...too relaxed.'

'What the hell's wrong with feeling relaxed, Georgia?' Mac couldn't believe she was doing this, backing away just when he was sure that he had won her back, sure that she too had felt how right they were together. 'You can't be *too relaxed*!'

'You would think that,' Georgia snapped, unnerved by the bitterness of his reaction. 'You've taken relaxation to an art form, but some of us have a sense of responsibility. I should never have exposed Toby to that...that...'

'That kiss?' Mac finished the sentence for her in a hard voice. 'It's not a dirty word, Georgia! And it's not a dirty deed. Toby's not bothered. He can't imagine why you would want to kiss anyone like that, but he's only eight. One day he'll learn, but he won't have a clue if you try and protect him from seeing so much as a kiss. Surely it's good for him to see adults being affectionate together?'

Georgia coloured. 'We were being a bit more than affectionate.'

'Yes, we were being loving,' said Mac pointedly. 'It's what makes life worth living. Ideally, you don't want an audience, I agree, but it wasn't the end of the world, was it?'

Forcing the tension from his shoulders, he

walked over to where Georgia was still standing tautly by the door. 'We haven't got an audience now,' he reminded her, reaching for her hands, but she snatched them away.

'No, Mac. I'm sorry, really sorry, if I seemed encouraging earlier, but I've had second thoughts,' she said as steadily as she could. 'It would be a mistake if—'

'If what? If you took a chance, for once in your life? If you believed in me? If you believed in love?' Mac was gripped by a corrosive mixture of anger, frustration and bitter disappointment. 'You've spent a lot of time telling me that you've changed in the last four years, Georgia, but you haven't. You haven't changed at all. You're still the same old Georgia—afraid of life, afraid of love.'

'I've got good reason to be!' Georgia's temper flared. 'I took a risk loving you, and in the end it hurt—it hurt so much I could hardly breathe. I can't go through that again.'

Mac sighed. 'What can I do, other than promise you that it won't be like that this time round? You've made me jump through hoops, prove that I can think about you and what you need, and it's still not enough for you. It's never going to be enough, is it? Because you're scared,' he said. 'You're scared of loving, scared of losing control over your tidy little life. You'd rather be safe and have every 'i' dotted, every 't' neatly crossed, than let a little mess, a little compromise, into your life! You're so scared, you're rather be miserable and tidy on your own than happy and messy with someone else!'

'That's on the assumption that I can only be happy with you,' said Georgia furiously. 'You can be so arrogant sometimes, Mac, it's unbelievable! You're a fine one to talk to me about control! The only reason you're so angry now is because I won't go to bed with you when *you* want. Well, I'm sorry, but I don't feel like it.

'You've tried to change me ever since you met me,' she swept on accusingly. 'You wanted me to be a free spirit. You wanted me to be like you, in fact, and I'm not. I'm a nit-picking perfectionist with an obsessive desire for order, OK? That's who I *am*, and if you had ever bothered to look at me properly, to see me for what I am, instead of trying to make me into someone *you* want me to be, you'd know that.'

How had it all turned so nasty so quickly? Georgia wondered miserably as the days dragged past. One minute she was in Mac's arms, the next they were tearing each other apart. It was just like being married again. They couldn't carry on like this. Surely now Mac would have to accept that it was never going to work, and go?

But Mac said nothing, and Georgia had no choice but to carry on. She could have done without the charity ball the following Saturday, which was all anyone seemed to talk about that week. Why had she ever thought that it would be a good idea to go? If it hadn't been her suggestion, she would have been tempted to cry off. She was pretty sure that Geoffrey wouldn't mind. He hated dancing. But in the end, her pride wouldn't let her slink home and hide while the others were all out enjoying themselves. The *Gazette* was her paper, and there was no reason why she shouldn't go to the ball. Not going would only make Mac think that she was scared, and that was an accusation that had stung more than all the others.

She wasn't scared, Georgia told herself. Not only would she go to the ball, she would go and shine, and Mac would see that she was fine without him, just as she had said she would be.

Still, she was unprepared for the reaction when she turned up with Geoffrey at the Grand that Saturday evening. Kevin's jaw dropped and Niles's seedy eyes brightened with a new interest, while Cassie's stare was downright envious.

'Wow, you look incredible!' she said. 'Where did you get that *dress*?'

Georgia had, in fact, taken an unheard-of half day off and been all the way to Leeds for her outfit, determined to find a dress that would show Mac just how much she had changed. There would be no more discreetly elegant outfits. She wanted to look different. She wanted sexy, she wanted stunning. She wanted the wow factor.

And this dress certainly had that. Georgia knew the moment she tried it on. It was a gorgeous pale blue colour that flattered her skin and fitted like the proverbial glove, clinging voluptuously to the curves of her body before falling in a sensuous sweep of material to her ankles. From the front it was beautifully, if classically, cut, with quite a high neckline and sheer three-quarter-length sleeves. The front looked like the old Georgia: classic, discreet, elegant.

But the back... From behind, the dress was daringly low-cut, exposing her slender golden back, and finishing in a contemporary version of a bustle, which the assistant assured her was incredibly sexy. At the last minute, though, Georgia had lost her nerve about having quite so much flesh on show and had swathed her shoulders in a sheer spangly stole and, judging by the reaction at the table, she was glad that she had. If they were that amazed by her front view, what would they say when she turned round?

'You look lovely,' Rose agreed as Georgia introduced Geoffrey around the table. 'You should wear your hair down more often. It makes you look much younger.'

'Why, thank you, Rose,' said Georgia, touched. She sat down next to Geoffrey, noticing that there were two empty seats on her right. No prizes for guessing who was late.

'We just need Mac now,' said Cassie, who had

brought along a serious-looking young man she introduced as Simon. 'Oh, there he is now…' She waved. 'Mac, over here!'

In spite of her best efforts to fix a coolly un-interested expression on her face, Georgia's heart jerked at the mere sound of Mac's name. She had hardly seen him since he had walked out the pre-vious Saturday, and she was sure that he'd been avoiding her. He wasn't going to like finding him-self sitting next to her, but that was his fault for being late, wasn't it?

'Oh, and that's Frances with him,' said Rose, peering round Kevin to see where Cassie was looking. 'Doesn't she look nice?'

Geoffrey was talking to Niles across her, and Georgia allowed herself an oh-so-casual glance sideways to follow Cassie and Rose's gaze. She saw Mac instantly and her mouth dried. He was looking devastating in a dinner jacket. The severe lines suited his rangy build and emphasised the powerful set of his shoulders, and the dazzling whiteness of his shirt beneath the bow-tie threw the strong planes of his face, the brownness of his skin and the blueness of his eyes, into almost star-tling relief.

There was no sign of an elderly widow, though. Georgia frowned slightly. An elegant woman of about her own age was walking close behind him…how rude. Why was she following Mac like that? And…hang on…why was Mac pausing to smile reassuringly at her? Why was he ushering her forward as he reached the table?

'Hello, everyone,' he said, smiling around the table. His eyes didn't even falter as they passed Georgia's face. 'This is Frances.'

Georgia's jaw hung open. She couldn't help it. *This* was Frances? This was no elderly lady. Close to, Georgia had a nasty feeling that Frances was even younger than she was. She was natural-looking, with warm brown eyes and a sweet expression.

Georgia leant across Geoffrey to whisper to Rose. 'I thought Frances was a widow?'

'She is,' Rose whispered back. 'It was a terrible tragedy. Steven was only in his mid-thirties when he died, and Frances was devastated. She absolutely adored him, and they had both hoped to have children. They'd just bought a bigger house, so she rattles around in it now, but can't bear to sell it either. That's why she lets out a room. I know she's enjoyed having Mac there, for the company as much as anything.' Rose shook her head. 'It's such a shame. She's *such* a lovely person.'

The worst thing was that Frances *was* lovely. She was warm and friendly and chatted comfortably with everyone, while Georgia sat feeling ridiculous and gaudy in her spectacular dress. Why hadn't she worn something appropriate like Frances? And why couldn't she be bubbly and vivacious and the sort of person everybody liked, instead of a nit-picking control freak?

Frances probably didn't mind a bit of clutter. She would probably say that it made a house look cosy and comfortable, Georgia thought glumly. No wonder Mac was enjoying living with her. She watched him smiling at Frances, and it was clear that he liked the other woman a lot.

He was not the only one. Geoffrey was looking positively smitten. He had already established that they had friends in common—this was Askerby, after all—and was gazing at Frances with exactly the same expression he had used to look at Georgia when they did their Latin revision together all those years ago.

To cap it all, Frances could cook.

'I've never tasted pastry like hers,' Mac told the table, ignoring Frances's blushing protestations. 'It's sublime, and as for her puddings... Well, all I can say is that if you can eat with Frances, you wouldn't waste your money on any Michelin-starred restaurants!'

Really?' Geoffrey nearly fell off his chair with excitement.

'Why don't you get Frances to write a cookery column for the *Gazette*?' Mac addressed Georgia directly for the first time that evening.

'Oh, no, really, I'm not that good...' said Frances, clearly embarrassed by all the attention. 'I'm not sure I could do anything like that.'

'Nonsense,' said Mac. 'Of course you could.'

'I'm sure you'd be marvellous,' Geoffrey added warmly.

Georgia's lips had tightened at the casual way they were handing out jobs on her newspaper, but when Mac turned to her and demanded to know whether she thought a cookery column by Frances was a good idea or not, she forced herself to smile. She didn't want to look jealous. Even if she was.

'I don't think we really want to talk about this now,' she said as pleasantly as she could. 'This is supposed to be a social occasion. But if you're interested in a column, Frances, come in and see me some time. We could certainly talk about it.'

'That's very nice of you,' said Frances, who seemed to appreciate her far more than either Mac or Geoffrey.

'Ah, here's the band,' said Mac, swinging round in his chair. 'Come on, Frances, let's dance.'

Georgia was conscious of a sick feeling in her stomach as she watched them go, but she didn't want anyone thinking that she cared. It was clear that the others were already wondering why she and Mac weren't talking to each other after he had gone to so much trouble to arrange her day at the spa, but fortunately they were all too tactful to ask.

Putting up her chin, Georgia squared her shoulders and smiled brilliantly at Geoffrey. 'Why don't we go and join them?'

Shrugging the stole from her shoulders, she dragged a reluctant Geoffrey on to the dance floor, unaware of the collective intake of breath from the table as the full glory of her back view was revealed, and intent only on showing Mac what a good time she was having.

The ball was a popular annual event, and she soon lost sight of Mac and Frances in the throng. She was left shuffling awkwardly around the floor with poor Geoffrey, who was obviously hating every minute of it, and she felt suddenly guilty. It wasn't fair to make him dance just to make a point to Mac. It smacked uncomfortably of using him.

It was not a nice thought. Geoffrey had been a good friend to her, and he deserved better than that, thought Georgia with compunction, knowing that things weren't going to work out between them, and probably would never have done, even if Mac hadn't come back. Deep down, she knew that she had been hiding behind the idea of a relationship with Geoffrey. It had been something to cling on to when the rest of her life threatened to teeter out of control, as it so often did when Mac was around.

Now was not the time, but Georgia suspected that Geoffrey himself would be not surprised or even particularly disappointed when she told him that she would rather that they stayed just friends. Judging by the way he had been looking at Frances, he might even be relieved.

It was a lowering thought. Georgia had the impression that Geoffrey had got rather carried away by memories of his youthful and unrequited passion for her, and that he was disappointed that the reality of her hadn't quite lived up to his expectations. She was no longer the shy and studious schoolgirl he remembered, but a woman who was crisp and competent—except in the kitchen, of course. Georgia always had the feeling that Geoffrey would rather he could look after her more. He really needed someone softer, gentler, who would admire him wholeheartedly. Someone like Frances, in fact.

Georgia's mouth twisted as she remembered how determined she had been to settle down and make a life with Geoffrey. She had craved the reassuring steadiness and stability he represented but would that have been what Geoffrey wanted? He had a very comfortable life as it was. Would he really have wanted to change it for one with a brisk wife and a small sullen boy?

Georgia thought not.

To Geoffrey's obvious relief, the song came to an end and Georgia took pity on him. 'Let's go back to the table,' she said, tucking an affectionate hand in his arm as they made their way back through the tables. She should be nicer to him.

He was a kind man, a good man, who would make someone a wonderful husband.

Just not her husband.

She already had a husband, although not for much longer probably, Georgia realised bleakly. She couldn't see Mac making much objection to signing the divorce papers now.

The band was in full swing now. Georgia danced with Kevin, then Cassie's friend, Simon, and then with Niles, which involved much backing away from his squeezing hands. The only man who didn't ask her to dance was Mac. He disappeared for a while to take portraits of the revellers and, when he returned, he seemed distracted and uncharacteristically morose.

Geoffrey and Frances, having discovered that neither really liked to dance, had swapped seats and were nose to nose, obviously hitting it off. Georgia felt a bit spare, but she kept a bright smile fixed to her face and laughed and chatted across the table so that nobody would think she was jealous.

Mac was doing a much less successful job of appearing not to mind being abandoned by his partner. The famously laid-back humour was absent, and he sat broodingly with his brows drawn together over his nose and his eyes on the fork he was playing with between his fingers.

So absorbed in his own thoughts did he seem that Georgia was completely unprepared when

Mac raised his eyes without warning and stared straight into hers. The blue intensity of his gaze was like a shock jarring through her, making her heart stumble and sucking the air out of her lungs until she felt quite dizzy.

'Dance with me,' he said abruptly and shoved back his chair.

Georgia gaped at him, completely thrown by the sudden movement.

The next moment a hard hand had closed around her wrist and was lifting her bodily out of her chair. Practically dragged on to the dance floor, Georgia still hadn't had time to remember to breathe before Mac swung her round into his arms and pulled her tight against him.

'What…?' It came out as a squeaky gasp, and she sucked in some air and tried again. 'What are you doing?'

'I wanted to dance with you,' he said curtly.

'It didn't occur to you to ask me first?'

'Would you have said yes?'

'Probably not, given the way you're behaving tonight,' said Georgia tartly. 'You've either ignored me or manhandled me, and I have to say I don't appreciate either approach!'

'I haven't ignored you,' said Mac in a low, angry voice. 'God, I wish I could have done! I haven't been able to take my eyes off you all night. I've watched every breath you've taken.'

He sounded furious, and Georgia drew back her

head to look at him curiously. It wasn't like Mac. Even during the worst of the arguments they had had when splitting up, he had always maintained a mocking humour that had driven her wild, especially when he made her laugh just when she was most cross.

There was no question of laughing now, though. Her brow puckered as she studied him. 'Are you OK, Mac?' she asked carefully.

'No, I'm not OK,' said Mac bitterly. 'I thought I was, right up until the moment I saw you tonight. I thought I was fine. I'd accepted that it was over the other night. It was clear then that you weren't really interested, and I didn't see any point in jumping over endless hurdles when you obviously had no intention of ever changing your mind.'

He had been so angry when he'd left that night, Mac remembered. He would leave Askerby, leave the *Gazette*, leave Georgia, since she patently didn't want him. And he didn't want her any more. He was sick of trying to convince her that he loved her. Furiously he'd reminded himself of all her faults: she was uptight, critical, brisk, over-demanding, an unreasonable perfectionist. What on earth had made him think he wanted to live with someone like that again?

If it hadn't been for the fact that he couldn't quite bring himself to concede victory and admit that she had won their bet after all, he would have been on his way back to London by now. He had only waited so as not to disappoint Frances, whom he had promised to bring to this wretched ball. That was what Mac had told himself anyway.

And then tonight he had walked up and seen Georgia with Geoffrey. Her hair fell around her face in loose waves and she had made up her eyes so that they looked huge and sultry. She looked beautiful. Beautiful and aloof, her prickles firmly in place.

Mac had done his best to resist her. He had tried to ignore her, just as he had said, but when he'd been dancing with Frances—poor Frances who hadn't really wanted to dance at all—he had been thrown by a glimpse of an extraordinarily sexy woman through the crowd in a backless dress the like of which had probably never been seen in Askerby before. It showed off a smooth, golden, gleaming back and emphasised the curves of her body with a witty bustle.

It took a woman supremely confident of herself and her sexuality to wear a dress like that. For Mac, that brief glance of her back had been charged with more eroticism than any full-fronted nude. He'd craned his neck, trying to see it again, but the woman had disappeared in the crowd... No, there she was again... Who *was* she?

Mac had watched as she turned, smiling up at her partner, and had seen with a shock that jolted through his entire body that it was Georgia.

CHAPTER TEN

MAC had missed a step, stumbled, stared, and stared again. *Georgia.* Now he thought about it, she had had some kind of scarf around her shoulders before, but still, he couldn't believe that he hadn't recognized his own wife.

It was almost as if he had never seen her before, as if he had been looking at her through a long-distance lens and had then suddenly zoomed to startling detail, to the curve of her mouth, the sweep of her lashes, the proud tilt of her head. They were all so Georgia, so familiar, and yet suddenly so new and strange.

Mac had felt jarred as he'd taken Frances back to the table. Sitting next to Georgia after that had been torture as he'd fought the urge to stand up and shout, This woman is *mine!*' He ached to touch her, and in the end he hadn't been able to bear it any longer. He just had to hold her, and now she was in his arms and he could smell her perfume, touch the warm, supple back beneath his palm, feel the quivering tension in her body as he held her close.

'Let's go, Georgia,' he said, his voice low and urgent. 'Let's go home and make love and remember how good it feels to be together, the way we're meant to be.'

Reaching for her hand, he started to pull her towards the door, reckless with the need to get her alone, because, if he didn't, he was going to peel that dress off her right there and then in the middle of the ballroom. He couldn't wait to kiss his way all over her, to run his hands over her body and make her sigh and shudder and shatter with pleasure the way he had used to be able to do.

Hazy with desire, Mac could only think about one thing. If only Georgia would let him love her, she would remember what he did. She would remember the glory they had always found together, the heart-stopping release, the heart-healing comfort of holding each other close afterwards, feeling as one.

'Mac, wait!' Georgia managed to wrench her hand out of his grasp at last. 'Stop it!'

The look on her face snapped Mac to reality. 'Why do you keep fighting it, Georgia?' he demanded. 'Why can't you just give in and accept that we're meant to be together? You know it's true.'

'There's a chemistry between us, that's all.' Georgia felt absurdly shaken. She had felt the force of his need, almost frightening in its power, but really, what was he *thinking*?

'It's more than chemistry,' he said. 'It's love.'

'Mac…' she said in despair. 'We can't talk about this now.'

'I agree,' he said flatly. 'We've done enough talking. It's time for you to make up your mind, Georgia. I'm not going to jump through any more hoops for you. We've wasted enough time as it is. If you love me, come with me now, but if you want to carry on pretending that what we have isn't special, then you'd better scuttle back to Geoffrey.'

Georgia stared at him, too exasperated with him for choosing a place like this to put her on the spot, to care about the interest they were undoubtedly creating. A nice embarrassing scene that everyone could talk about for the next year was all that was needed to make the ball a rip-roaring success, and it looked as if she and Mac were set to provide it this year.

'There's no point in bandying around ultimatums, Mac,' she said sharply. 'I can't go with you now, even if I wanted to. I came here with Geoffrey. I can't just take off with you just because you've had enough. And you've got a partner too, in case you've forgotten,' she went on remorselessly. 'Were you planning to leave Frances high and dry?'

Mac expelled a sharp breath of sheer frustration. He had indeed forgotten about Frances. He had been so overwhelmed by his need for Georgia that he couldn't think straight.

'I've got a babysitter to pay when I get home,' Georgia swept on, determined to ram the point home. 'Should I just leave her in charge of Toby all night, and assume she won't mind being stuck in a strange house without pay? Oh, and who cares if her parents worry about where she is when I promised that I would put her in a taxi and send her home by midnight and she doesn't appear?

'That's typical of you, Mac,' she said, deliberately stoking her own anger to stop herself thinking about how good it would have felt to have slipped away with him, out of the ballroom, out of the hotel, to somewhere dark and quiet where they could forget everything except the frantic clamouring of their bodies.

'You never *think*!' she told him. 'You're like a child. You see what you want and you charge after it without considering the consequences or the effect on other people. When are you going to grow up and accept that life just isn't that simple any more? The rest of us have other responsibilities and commitments and we can't just drop them when we feel like it, or when *you* feel like it!

'I mean, what exactly were you expecting me to do? Rush off into the night with you and make mad passionate love? And where were we going? To your room at Frances's house? A little tacky, given that you'd asked her out this evening, don't you think? I suppose we could have gone to my home and brushed past the babysitter,' Georgia said, her voice dripping with sarcasm. 'Or maybe you were planning to rent a hotel room? I'm not sure the Grand rent rooms by the hour, but I guess we could have found a tacky hotel somewhere and that would have made me feel *really* good!'

'All right,' said Mac, his jaw clenched with humiliation and fury. 'You've made your point. I'll take it,' he said, 'that your answer is no.'

He gave in his notice on Monday morning. 'You've won,' he said. 'Congratulations.'

Georgia regarded him bleakly. She had never felt less like celebrating. 'When are you thinking of going?'

'Tomorrow.'

'So soon?' she said, unable to hide the flicker of dismay in her eyes.

'There's no point in me hanging around now, is there?' said Mac in the same hard voice. 'Don't worry, Gary will be able to carry on, at least for now. He's got a good eye.'

She had known that this would happen, Georgia reminded herself desolately. Right from the beginning, she had known that he would go and that it would hurt. It was for the best, perhaps, but she was still unprepared for the pain that gripped her heart in its savage claws. She had what felt like a knot of barbed wire inside her, and every time she moved it tore agonisingly at her.

'Will you say goodbye to Toby?'

'Of course.' Now that the arguments were over, they could be meticulously polite to each other. 'I thought I'd go and meet him from school this afternoon, if that's OK with you.'

Georgia had to clasp her hands together on her desk to stop them shaking. 'I'll let the school know,' she said. 'He'll be sorry to see you go,' she added with an effort and then made herself ask the question she dreaded. 'Will...will I see you again?'

'Of course.' Mac bared his teeth. 'I need to sign those divorce papers, don't I? I'll wait with Toby until you get home tonight.'

Georgia didn't know whether to be glad or sorry that she had a lunch meeting with Griff Carver that day. The *Gazette* seemed to be the least of her worries right then, but what was the alternative? To sit here in dumb misery, knowing that there was absolutely nothing she could do to make things better. Ever since Mac had reappeared, she had felt like a rabbit stuck in the headlights, unable to get out of the way and save herself from the pain she had known was coming. And now it had finally hit her, it was, in an odd way, something of a relief not to be dreading how much it would hurt any more.

So she put on her lipstick and went out to Griff Carver's palatial home outside Askerby and closed her mind to anything except the *Gazette*. She wouldn't think about Mac, about the bitterness in his face or how empty her life was going to be when he had gone. She would just think about advertising revenue and sales figures and budgets.

Griff had the ability to focus completely, and that helped too. He kept her there all afternoon, going through the accounts, reviewing what seemed like every edition and discussing options for the future. It was very intensive, but Georgia didn't care as long as it stopped her thinking about anything else. She knew that Toby was with Mac, and the longer she was holed up in this meeting, the less time she would have to face saying goodbye.

It was nearly half past five before Griff let her go, and Georgia was exhausted. She had hardly slept the last two nights, and it felt as if a steel band was tightening around her head. She would just check her messages at the office, and then she would go home.

Rose had gone by the time she got back to the office, and the newsroom was empty. There was a note on her desk, which Rose had starred and marked 'urgent'. Mac, she had written, had been trying to ring Georgia's mobile all afternoon. If she got the message before he reached her, could she ring him back straight away? 'Straight away' was underlined three times.

'I've been trying to get hold of you all afternoon,' he said furiously when Georgia rang his mobile phone. 'Why didn't you answer?'

'I was in a meeting with Griff Carver, and he hates interruptions,' she said. 'I had to turn my phone off.'

'Where are you now?'

'At the office.'

'It's six o'clock,' Mac exploded. 'You shouldn't be at the office. You should be at home. Toby needs you.'

Georgia went cold all over. 'What's happened? Is he ill?'

'No, he's not ill, but he's in trouble,' said Mac grimly. 'The police picked him up for shoplifting at lunchtime.'

Georgia got home in record time. 'Where's Toby?' she asked Mac who was waiting alone in the living room.

'He's in his room.'

She turned for the stairs, but Mac caught her arm. 'Wait! He's dreading seeing you. Don't rush up and shout at him.'

'I wasn't going to shout at him,' said Georgia, icy with rage, as she wrenched her arm out of his grasp.

'What were you going to do?'

'I don't know,' she admitted, her fury subsiding as quickly as it had arisen. 'I just wanted to see how he was.'

'Well, I suggest you sit down first and find out what happened,' said Mac.

He waited until Georgia had sat in the armchair and then told her the little that he knew. Toby, it seemed, was being bullied.

'I suppose it was inevitable,' he said. 'Toby's a clever child, and a bit geeky, and also he's different. He hasn't got any parents, and he lives with a woman who managed to alienate whole sections of the town by getting the previous editor of the *Gazette* sacked.'

Georgia flushed and set her teeth. 'I knew he wasn't particularly happy at school, but he'd never talk about it.'

'You don't when you're being bullied. You're too scared to say anything.'

'I should have known, though.' She twisted her fingers together guiltily. 'How did he end up stealing?'

'The boys who were bullying him made him go and get some sweets for them in the lunch break. Poor Toby didn't have any money and they were standing outside, waiting for him. Of course the newsagent saw what he was doing and called the police. Toby wouldn't say anything, but fortunately the policeman had a pretty good idea of what was going on. He gave Toby a talking-to, which will probably make him law-abiding for life, and took him back to the school, who, of course, tried to ring you.'

Mac paused. 'I just happened to answer the phone when the headteacher rang the newsroom trying to track you down. She recognized my name, as you'd already told her that I'd be picking Toby up this afternoon, so I went along early to see him.'

'How was he?' asked Georgia, cursing herself for turning her mobile off. She should have insisted to Griff that she could take urgent calls.

'Scared, although more of the bullies than the police,' said Mac. 'He wouldn't say anything at first, but I managed to get the story out of him and I think the headteacher is going to deal with the bullying. No doubt you'll want to talk to her yourself—if you can spare the time from your precious newspaper, of course,' he added abrasively. 'Who knows, it might make a nice headline-grabbing article for you. 'Schoolboy in Shoplifting Scandal', perhaps.'

Georgia flinched. 'That's not fair!'

'Isn't it? You've had a lot to say about how irresponsible I am, Georgia, but maybe it's time you took a long, hard look at yourself. You may be grown up and drive around in a sensible car and wear sensible clothes and want to hang around with sensible people like Geoffrey, but how responsible is it to take charge of a small boy and then dump him in an after school club where he gets bullied so that you can get on with your career?'

'Hold on—' Georgia began, outraged, but Mac swept on.

'You spend all that extra time at the *Gazette*, caring about how exciting and innovative it is, when that's time you could be spending with Toby. And if you had ever been bothered to spend time talking to him, finding out what he thinks and feels, and whether he's happy, you might have known about the bullying before now and done something to help him. But no! Georgia Maitland is much too important to waste her time doing that kind of thing! You've got a career, as you reminded me endlessly when we discussed having a family, and that was always going to come before some child. You obviously haven't changed your mind since then.'

'How dare you?' Georgia surged to her feet, white-faced with fury. 'How *dare* you lecture me about responsibility, Mac? I gave up my job and my home and my life in London for Toby! When have you ever given up anything for anybody?'

It was her turn to brush aside his attempt to answer. 'Oh, sure it made you feel good to cruise into school today and act all concerned. Quite the hero, weren't you? But the fact is that you don't know anything about bringing up a child. I may not know much, but I know more than you. I care for Toby the best I possibly I can, and I certainly don't need any lectures from *you* about being responsible. In fact,' she finished vehemently, 'I don't need anything from you, and nor does Toby!'

'In that case, where are those divorce papers?' said Mac, biting out each word. 'Since I'm not needed, I might as well sign now.'

'Good idea.' Her face taut with anger, Georgia found the papers and slapped them down on the table. 'Here's a pen,' she said, and pointed. 'You need to sign there.'

Taking the pen from her with a glance of dislike, Mac scrawled his name and then tossed the pen contemptuously on to the table.

'That's it then,' he said. 'Enjoy your nice safe life.'

And then he picked up his jacket and his camera and walked out.

Georgia stood stock still. She heard the door open and then slam shut, and then, without warning, she bent double as the pain hit her like a kick in the stomach. Clutching her arms around her, she fought for breath. She was *not* going to cry, not now. She could cry later, thinking about the dislike and contempt in Mac's eyes as he signed away their marriage at last, but for now Toby came first.

She climbed the stairs slowly, like an old lady.

Toby was sitting on his bed, hugging his knees, curling up to make himself as small as possible. He glanced up at Georgia as she came in, and then buried his face back in his knees without a word.

Georgia went over and sat next to him, putting her arm around the thin shoulders.

'Sorry.' Toby's voice was muffled, but she heard him and her throat closed.

'I'm sorry too, Toby,' she said. 'I should have been here.'

'Mac was there, but now he's gone away,' muttered Toby. 'Is it because of what I did?'

'No, oh, *no*, Toby!' Georgia said, horrified. 'Of course not. Mac wouldn't do that. It's nothing to do with you, I promise.'

Toby lifted a tear-stained face. 'Then why's he gone?' he asked, his voice cracking, and Georgia swallowed.

'He's gone because of me. It's my fault, Toby,' she said, and then she too began to cry.

The package arrived the following Saturday. 'It's a camera!' said Toby, tearing open the paper. 'It's from Mac!'

Georgia stared down at the bulky folder that had been addressed to her. Very slowly, she opened it, and pulled out a card. *This is the Georgia I saw*, was all it said.

'What is it?' asked Toby curiously.

'They're photographs,' said Georgia in an odd voice.

Toby came round to peer over her shoulder. 'They're all of you!'

She hadn't realised Mac had taken so many pictures of her. Half the time, she hadn't even noticed when he was clicking away with his camera, but he had noticed her. There were photos of her when they were first married, in Africa, looking achingly young and blissfully happy, and then in London. Georgia in her neat suit, Georgia asleep in bed, her arm thrown over her head and her hair tumbled over her face. Georgia laughing, Georgia frowning, Georgia peering dubiously at something she had just taken out of the oven. Georgia looking flirtatious, Georgia being brisk and efficient.

And then there were photos of her in Askerby. Picking up Toby's toys—when had he taken *that?*—or in the newsroom, looking over her glasses as she talked to someone out of the shot. Curled defensively up on the sofa. At the ball, in that dress, looking alluring.

There was a hard lump in Georgia's throat. Mac had captured her essence. He had seen her in a way that no one else ever had. The photographs were taken with love, that much was obvious, but it was a clear-sighted rather than a besotted love. True, some of the pictures made her look beautiful, but in others she seemed tired and harassed. They showed her as a real woman, with all the contradictions that made her uniquely Georgia—strong and yet vulnerable, sexy and practical, warm but wary.

She had been wrong when she had accused Mac of not knowing her, Georgia realised. He knew her better than she knew herself.

Beside her, Toby sighed. 'I miss Mac.'

Afterwards, Georgia would wonder at herself. She had spent her whole life being careful and sensible and thinking things through, and now, suddenly, the knowledge of what she had to do possessed her so strongly that she didn't even stop to consider the consequences.

Picking up the phone, she rang the Picture Editor of the national newspaper who had used Mac's work for many years. 'Yes, he's off on an assignment—today, in fact, Georgia,' he said cheerfully after an exchange of pleasantries on either side. 'He came in last week and asked if I had any work for him. I'd thought he'd given up overseas work, so I was really glad to see him. You don't turn down the chance of pictures by Mac Henderson, do you?'

'Where's he going?' asked Georgia, hoping that he couldn't hear the tension in her voice.

'Burkina Faso.'

Burkina Faso! Her heart sank. He couldn't have found somewhere more difficult for her to follow him? 'And he's gone already?'

'His flight's tonight, I think.' There was some rustling of papers. 'Yes, six-thirty... Looks like you've missed him. If he calls me before he goes, do you want me to tell him you're trying to get in touch with him?'

'No, don't do that,' said Georgia, looking at her watch. Mac would have to check in at four thirty. That gave her just under six hours to get to Heathrow. Say three and a bit hours to London on the train, allowing for a connection in York, an hour to get out to the airport... Plenty of time. 'I'll tell him myself.'

Come on...come *on*,' Georgia muttered as the Piccadilly line train crept into another station and shuddered to a halt. What was taking so long? Everything seemed to be happening in slow motion today. The doors would sigh open with excruciating slowness at each station, only to take even longer to close again, while the train stopped in every tunnel, as if afraid of the light at the other end.

Her six hours were up. Everything had started so auspiciously too. Rose had heard the urgency in her voice and calmly agreed to have Toby for the day without even asking where Georgia was going. 'Just drop him on your way to the station,' she said.

Georgia had caught the train to York by the skin of her teeth, which meant she had been able to fall into a seat on the London train with a sigh of relief, congratulating herself on having made it.

Too soon, as it turned out. Signal problems and a broken-down train on the line ahead meant that they had been over an hour late arriving at King's Cross, and now she was stuck on this stupid tube, which was obviously going for the record for the slowest ever journey out to Heathrow Airport. With every chance of winning.

South Ealing...NorthFields...Boston Manor... Georgia stared out at the platform signs in an agony of impatience. It was already nearly five o'clock, and her stomach was churning with desperation. She was going to be late. She was going to miss him. He would go off to Burkina Faso and never come back, and she would have lost her chance to tell him that she was sorry and that she missed him, so much more than Toby did.

Georgia's only hope was that Mac would be late, as usual. If she had been booked on a flight to Burkina Faso, she would panic unless she could check in and go through Passport Control with a good three hours to spare, a habit that had driven Mac wild whenever they had travelled together, but she was banking on his much more casual approach now.

At last! Georgia leapt out of the train and ran along the seemingly endless underground tunnels that led to Terminal Three, careless of the curious looks as she struggled on, bright red, wheezing, plait coming apart so that she had to keep brushing it frantically away from her face.

She had this terrible image of Mac, camera bag on his shoulder, strolling towards Passport Control, showing his boarding card, handing over his passport, disappearing into the Departure Lounge... And then what would she do? Go tamely back to Askerby? She could get the next plane to Burkina Faso, Georgia thought wildly, but that might be days... Oh, please, *please*, be late, Mac!

Oh, thank God, there was the gate into the Departure Lounge! Passengers were queuing patiently on the long ramp leading down to where boarding cards were being checked, before the line snaked on to Passport Control. If Mac hadn't been through yet, she would catch him here. It was her last—her only—chance.

Georgia panted to a halt, practically bent double as she struggled for breath. Really, she was going to have to make time to go to the gym. All around her were couples taking loving farewells, and families seeing off relatives with hugs and tears. Pushing her way through them to the rail so that she could get a better view of the queue, Georgia searched the line with her eyes, just in case Mac had had a personality transformation and decided to check in more than two minutes before take-off and—dear God, there he was! Her heart stopped at the sight of that familiar, rangy figure, moving inexorably towards the front of the queue.

'Mac!' she called, but it came out as little more than a wheeze. There was no way he would be able to hear her. Georgia coughed desperately to clear her throat. 'Mac!' she tried again.

One or two people at the back of the queue turned to look at her, but she wasn't interested in them. Mac was almost at the gate. He had his boarding card ready to hand to the official. Georgia stopped, forcing herself to take slow, deep breaths before she filled her lungs for a last try.

Mac!' she yelled.

The entire terminal seemed to stop, heads turning towards her as if pulled by a single string, but for Georgia there was only one pair of eyes staring at her that counted. Mac had seen her.

She waved feebly. 'Mac,' she whispered, unable to think of anything else to say.

For one terrible moment, she thought that he was just going to turn away, show his boarding card and disappear into the departure lounge, but then he turned and began shouldering his way back along the queue towards her, ignoring the amused looks he was getting.

'Excuse me…sorry…excuse me,' she could hear him muttering, until he finally fought his way back to where she was standing and stopped about three feet away.

Georgia was so relieved to have caught him in time that she felt almost faint at the narrowness of her escape, and she clutched at the rail for support. She was still puffing and panting from her desperate run from the tube, and she was horribly conscious of how she must look—a mad middle-aged woman with a pink face and hair all over the place.

'Georgia?' said Mac.

'I…I wanted to catch you before you went,' she gasped.

'I gathered that.' The corner of his mouth twitched slightly. 'Don't you think you could have shouted a bit louder? I think there are several million people in New York who didn't quite hear you!'

'I'm sorry…' Georgia made herself take another deep breath to try and calm her hammering lungs. 'I just didn't want you to go without telling you…I need to talk to you… It's just…' Oh, God, why hadn't she thought about what she was going to say while she was stuck on that wretched train. 'When do you have to board?'

Mac glanced at the departure board above their heads, where a green light was flashing next to his flight number. 'Now,' he said.

'Oh, then there's no time…' said Georgia wretchedly, but Mac just took her arm and steered her over to some uncomfortable seats upholstered in a particularly unattractive shade of purple.

'There's time,' he said. 'And, as you seem to have made a huge effort to get here in time, you might as well tell me what you came to say.'

Georgia's legs seemed to buckle and she collapsed on to the seat. Every fibre of her body had been straining to reach him in time and now that he was there she felt ridiculously shy. Rather too late, she remembered the bitterness in his face as he had left that day, the terrible things they had said to each other, and all at once it seemed as if she had been appallingly presumptuous in thinking that he would want to hear what she had to say.

But she had come this far, so she might as well go on.

She licked her dry lips. 'I wanted...I wanted to thank you,' she said.

'*Thank* me?' said Mac incredulously. It was the last thing he had expected her to say after the way he had treated her. 'What on earth for?'

'For all you did for Toby,' she said. 'And for everything you did for the *Gazette*, but most of all for reminding me what it feels like to be truly alive again.'

Taking another deep breath, Georgia looked into his face, painful honesty in her grey eyes. 'And I wanted to say that I'm sorry, Mac. I'm sorry for the things I said to you, sorry because I disappointed you, and sorry because I lied. I let you think that you had lost that bet we made when I knew that really you had won.'

Something flickered deep in Mac's navy blue gaze. 'I convinced you that I loved you?'

'Yes, you did.' She squared her shoulders. 'You were right about something else, too,' she said. 'You were right when you said that I still loved you, but I was too afraid to put my heart on the line again and, because I was scared, I lost my chance to be happy again. I wish I hadn't,' she burst out, the words tumbling out so fast now that she hardly knew what she was saying. 'I don't know why I came really. I know I've left it too late, and I understand if you don't want to bother any more. It's just…'

'Just what?' asked Mac gently.

'It's just that I can't bear the thought of life without you again.' To her horror, Georgia felt her eyes fill with tears. 'I had four years of missing you. I know what it's like to wake every single morning and feel that lead weight in my stomach because you're not there. I remember that horrible sense that all the joy has trickled out of life. I'd look out at a sunny day and just feel flat and bleak and empty without you.'

She swallowed. 'I know what it's like to walk around hunched up against the terrible pain in my heart. It was like an awful crack that wouldn't heal, that stayed raw for four long years so that every time I thought of you, it hurt so much I could hardly breathe.'

'And then, just when I was beginning to be able to bear it after all, you came to Askerby,' she said. 'I couldn't face it starting all over again. I did everything I could to stop it. You were right; I tried to hide away. I was too afraid of hurting like that again to realise that I was being offered a second chance, that I could have been happy again, so I threw it away.'

She stopped, biting fiercely down on her bottom lip to stop it trembling, and stared at a couple locked in each other's arms, oblivious to the rest of the world as they said goodbye.

'I know it's too late now,' she said, drawing a ragged breath, 'but I want you to know that you were right. I do love you, I've always loved you, and I'll never love anyone else.'

She pulled out the envelope, battered now after being to Africa and back, and now stuffed into her bag at the last minute for a final journey down to London. 'These are the papers you signed. Take them if you want them, and send them off, and then the divorce will go through. I don't want to do it myself.'

'I see.' Mac nodded thoughtfully and held out his hand. 'In that case, I'll take them now.'

Well, what had she expected? He had offered her his love, and she had had plenty of chances to take it, only to waste every one. She had left it too late to change her mind. Sick at heart, Georgia put the envelope in his hand with a dull sense of inevitability.

Mac drew out the papers and looked through them. 'Just as well to check,' he said. 'Yes, this seems to be our divorce, all signed and ready to go.'

And then, very slowly and deliberately, he tore them up.

Uncomprehending, Georgia watched the pieces of paper scatter on the carpet, before she raised her eyes back to Mac's face.

'Don't tell me,' said Mac. 'I've made a mess.'

Georgia's mouth wobbled. 'Mac…' she said, uncertain whether to laugh or cry.

'Well, since you love me and I love you, there doesn't seem much point in getting divorced, does there?' he said reasonably.

'No.' Eyes starry with tears, she reached for him. 'Not when you put it like that.'

And then at last she was in his arms, and they were kissing each other with a kind of desperation. Georgia clung to him, hardly able to believe that he was real, and solid, and *there*, that he loved her still.

'I'm sorry, I'm sorry…' she gasped between kisses as the tears she had held back for so long spilt over at last. 'I'm sorry I was so horrible when you turned up in Askerby. I can't believe you can still love me when I'm so difficult, and so repressed about tidying up and such a terrible cook!'

'And such a bad driver,' added Mac, smiling as he held her tight. 'Don't forget that!'

'Well, exactly,' said Georgia with a watery sniff. 'Are you sure you can bear to live with me again?'

Mac held her away from him and took her face in his hands. 'The thing is, Georgia, you may be stubborn and stiff-necked and spiky, and, yes, more than a little repressed about punctuality and tidiness,' he said, and then his smile faded, leaving only the warmth and the truth in his blue eyes. 'But you're also beautiful and kind and honest and clever and warm and sexy, and the fact is that I can't bear *not* to live with you.

'I know what you mean about the emptiness of the last four years,' he went on, letting his hands slide lovingly down her throat, over her shoulders and down her arms to take both her hands in his. 'I know how bleak and meaningless life was for me too without you.'

His fingers tightened around hers. 'I was arrogant, just like you said I was, and I took you for granted—I see that now—but it was only when I lost you that I knew just how much I loved you, and what a fool I had been to let you go. I hurt you, Georgia, and I'm sorry, more sorry than I can say. I promise I'll never hurt you like that again.'

Georgia pulled one hand away to lay a finger against his lips. 'Promises can be dangerous things, Mac. We made a promise to each other when we married, and both of us broke that. We didn't mean to hurt each other, but we did. I think all we can promise now is that we'll try not to do it again.'

'You said you didn't want to take a risk on that,' Mac made himself remind her, and she nodded.

'I know I did, but if there's one thing I've learnt since you left Askerby, it's that I was wrong. You can't love if you don't make yourself vulnerable to being hurt. You can never guard yourself against that. Yes, things might go wrong again, but they certainly won't go right unless I *do* take that risk. I tried living without love, without risk, but that was living without you, and that's too high a price for me to pay for security.'

'What about Toby?' asked Mac. 'Are you really prepared to take a risk for him, too?'

'I think Toby would be furious if he thought I'd even considered not taking a risk on you because of him!' said Georgia ruefully. 'He likes you and he trusts you, and that means he'll learn from you how to take hold of life and live it to the full. That's a better role model for him than someone who'll always play it safe.'

Mac smiled, deeply pleased, and pulled her back against him. 'Talking of whom, does

Geoffrey know that you're here?' he said, kissing the curve of her shoulder, the place which always made her arch instinctively with a little shudder of pleasure.

'Not yet,' she managed, not without some difficulty as Mac's lips drifted higher up her throat. 'But I don't think he'll care. He came round after you left, wanting to tell me that he'd fallen madly in love with Frances.'

'Ah, my plan worked!' said Mac with satisfaction, and Georgia pulled away to look up at him.

'Plan?' she demanded suspiciously.

'Why do you think I invited Frances to the ball? She's a great person, and perfect for Geoffrey. My cunning plan was to find some way of introducing them and hope that Frances would lure Geoffrey away from you, so that I could step back into my rightful place by your side!'

'Oh, did you?' said Georgia with mock wrath, remembering how jealous she had been of Frances. 'And what if I hadn't chased you all the way to the airport this evening? You'd have gone off to Burkina Faso, leaving me high and dry in Askerby without even Geoffrey for support!'

Mac grinned. 'I'm only going for a week, Georgia. I think you could have managed that on your own!'

'A week! I thought you were going off for ever!'

'No.' He shook his head. 'Oh, I was pretty angry when I left, and I did have some high-minded thoughts about never going back, but it was soon obvious that wouldn't have worked. I missed Askerby too much. I missed the *Gazette* and photographing retiring scout masters. I missed Toby. But most of all,' he said, his voice very deep and low as he held her close, 'I missed you, Georgia. I don't know what it is, but the light's just not the same when you're not there.'

He kissed her then, a long, slow, sweet kiss that dissolved the last of Georgia's doubts and confusions and left her feeling giddy with the glorious sense of having reached a safe port after a long and treacherous voyage alone.

'I love you,' he said, as a tannoy above their heads announced the final call for passengers boarding the flight to Ouagadougou.

'Is that your flight?' asked Georgia, distracted in spite of herself, and Mac laughed out loud.

'I wondered how long it would take before your plane fever kicked in!'

'You'll miss it if you're not careful!'

'I'll go if you'll tell me that you love me too, and that you'll be waiting for me when I get back next week!'

Georgia smiled. 'Toby and I will both be waiting for you,' she promised. 'We'll always be there for you.'

'And...?' Mac prompted.

'And I love you too,' she said, kissing him

softly. 'Very much. Now go, or you'll miss that plane!'

He kissed her once more, a fierce kiss of possession and promise, and then he turned and walked back down to rejoin the queue for the Departure Lounge. As he handed over his boarding card, he turned and smiled back at Georgia, who touched her fingers to her lips to blow her husband a kiss, her eyes shining.

She watched him out of sight, and then she turned to go. The divorce papers were still scattered over the carpet where Mac had dropped them. Georgia stopped and picked them up. No doubt Mac would roll his eyes, but he knew she didn't like leaving a mess.

Smiling, she looked down at her divorce in pieces in her hands for a long moment, before she dumped it in the bin and headed back to Askerby.

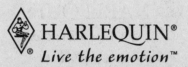

HARLEQUIN® _Super_ROMANCE®

...there's more to the story!

Superromance.
A *big* satisfying read about unforgettable
characters. Each month we offer *six* very different
stories that range from family drama to adventure
and mystery, from highly emotional stories to
romantic comedies—and much more! Stories
about people you'll believe in and care about.
Stories too compelling to put down....

Our authors are among today's *best* romance
writers. You'll find familiar names and talented
newcomers. Many of them are award winners—
and you'll see why!

If you want the biggest and best
in romance fiction, you'll get it
from Superromance!

Emotional, Exciting, Unexpected...

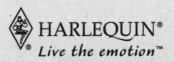

HARLEQUIN®
Live the emotion™

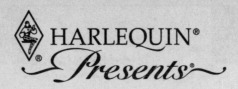

HARLEQUIN®
Presents

The world's bestselling romance series...
The series that brings you your favorite authors,
month after month:

Helen Bianchin...Emma Darcy
Lynne Graham...Penny Jordan
Miranda Lee...Sandra Marton
Anne Mather...Carole Mortimer
Susan Napier...Michelle Reid

and many more uniquely talented authors!

Wealthy, powerful, gorgeous men...
Women who have feelings just like your own...
The stories you love, set in exotic, glamorous locations...

HARLEQUIN®
Presents

Seduction and Passion Guaranteed!

HPDIR104

Harlequin Historicals®
Historical Romantic Adventure!

From rugged lawmen and valiant knights to defiant heiresses and spirited frontierswomen, Harlequin Historicals will capture your imagination with their dramatic scope, passion and adventure.

Harlequin Historicals . . . they're too good to miss!

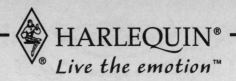

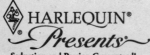

HARLEQUIN®
INTRIGUE®

WE'LL LEAVE YOU BREATHLESS!

If you've been looking for thrilling tales of
contemporary passion and sensuous love stories
with taut, edge-of-the-seat suspense—then
you'll love Harlequin Intrigue!

Every month, you'll meet six new heroes
who are guaranteed to make your spine tingle
and your pulse pound. With them you'll enter
into the exciting world of Harlequin Intrigue—
where your life is on the line
and so is your heart!

THAT'S INTRIGUE—
ROMANTIC SUSPENSE
AT ITS BEST!

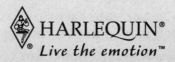

HARLEQUIN®
Live the emotion™